ACROSS THE YEARS
BY
ELEANOR H. PORTER

ACROSS THE YEARS BY ELEANOR H. PORTER

When Father and Mother Rebelled

"'Tain't more 'n a month ter Christmas, Lyddy Ann; did ye know it?" said the old man, settling back in his chair with a curiously resigned sigh.

"Yes, I know, Samuel," returned his wife, sending a swift glance over the top of her glasses.

If Samuel Bertram noticed the glance he made no sign. "Hm!" he murmured. "I've got ten neckerchiefs now. How many crocheted bed-slippers you got?--eh?"

"Oh, Samuel!" remonstrated Lydia Ann feebly.

"I don't care," asserted Samuel with sudden vehemence, sitting erect in his chair. "Seems as if we might get somethin' for Christmas 'sides slippers an' neckerchiefs. Jest 'cause we ain't so young as we once was ain't no sign that we've lost all our faculty for enj'yment!"

"But, Samuel, they're good an' kind, an' want ter give us somethin'," faltered Lydia Ann; "and--"

"Yes, I know they're good an' kind," cut in Samuel wrathfully. "We've got three children, an' each one brings us a Christmas present ev'ry year. They've got so they do it reg'lar now, jest the same as they--they go ter bed ev'ry night," he finished, groping a little for his simile. "An' they put jest about as much thought into it, too," he added grimly.

"My grief an' conscience, Samuel,--how can you talk so!" gasped the little woman opposite.

"Well, they do," persisted Samuel. "They buy a pair o' slippers an' a neckerchief, an' tuck 'em into their bag for us--an' that's done; an' next year they do the same--an' it's done again. Oh, I know I'm ongrateful, an' all that," acknowledged Samuel testily, "but I can't help it. I've been jest ready to bile over ever since last Christmas, an' now I have biled over. Look a-here, Lyddy Ann, we ain't so awful old. You're seventy-three an' I'm seventy-six, an' we're pert as sparrers, both of us. Don't we live here by ourselves, an' do most all the work inside an' outside the house?"

"Yes," nodded Lydia Ann timidly.

"Well, ain't there somethin' you can think of sides slippers you'd like for Christmas--'specially as you never wear crocheted bed-slippers?"

Lydia Ann stirred uneasily. "Why, of course, Samuel," she began hesitatingly, "bed-slippers are very nice, an'--"

"So's codfish!" interrupted Samuel in open scorn. "Come," he coaxed, "jest supposin' we was youngsters again, a-tellin' Santa Claus what we wanted. What would you ask for?"

Lydia Ann laughed. Her cheeks grew pink, and the lost spirit of her youth sent a sudden sparkle to her eyes. "You'd laugh, dearie. I ain't a-goin' ter tell."

"I won't--'pon honor!"

"But it's so silly," faltered Lydia Ann, her cheeks a deeper pink. "Me-- an old woman!"

"Of course," agreed Samuel promptly. "It's bound ter be silly, ye know, if we want anythin' but slippers an' neckerchiefs," he added with a chuckle. "Come--out with it, Lyddy Ann."

"It's--it's a tree."

"Dampers and doughnuts!" ejaculated Samuel, his jaw dropping. "A tree!"

"There, I knew you'd laugh," quavered Lydia Ann, catching up her knitting.

"Laugh? Not a bit of it!" averred Samuel stoutly. "I--I want a tree myself!"

"Ye see, it's just this," apologized Lydia Ann feverishly. "They give us things, of course, but they never make anythin' of doin' it, not even ter tyin' 'em up with a piece of red ribbon. They just slip into our bedroom an' leave 'em all done up in brown paper an' we find 'em after they're gone. They mean it all kind, but I'm so tired of gray worsted and sensible things. Of course I can't have a tree, an' I don't suppose I really want it; but I'd like somethin' all pretty an' sparkly an'--an' silly, you know. An' there's another thing I want--ice cream. An' I want to make myself sick eatin' it, too,--if I want to; an' I want little pink-an'-white sugar pep'mints hung in bags. Samuel, can't you see how pretty a bag o' pink pep'mints 'd be on that green tree? An'--dearie me!" broke off the little old woman breathlessly, falling back in her chair. "How I'm runnin' on! I reckon I am in my dotage."

For a moment Samuel did not reply. His brow was puckered into a prodigious frown, and his right hand had sought the back of his head--as was always the case when in deep thought. Suddenly his face cleared.

"Ye ain't in yer dotage--by gum, ye ain't!" he cried excitedly. "An' I ain't, neither. An' what's more, you're a-goin' ter have that tree--ice cream, pink pep'mints, an' all!"

"Oh, my grief an' conscience--Samuel!" quavered Lydia Ann.

"Well, ye be. We can do it easy, too. We'll have it the night 'fore Christmas. The children don't get here until Christmas day, ever, ye know, so 't won't interfere a mite with their visit, an' 'twill be all over 'fore they get here. An' we'll make a party of it, too," went on Samuel gleefully. "There's the Hopkinses an' old Mis' Newcomb, an' Uncle Tim, an' Grandpa Gowin'--they'll all come an' be glad to."

"Samuel, could we?" cried Lydia Ann, incredulous but joyous. "Could we, really?"

"I'll get the tree myself," murmured Samuel, aloud, "an' we can buy some o' that shiny stuff up ter the store ter trim it."

"An' I'll get some of that pink-an'-white tarl'tan for bags," chimed in Lydia Ann happily: "the pink for the white pep'mints, an' the white for the pink. Samuel, won't it be fun?" And to hear her one would have thought her seventeen instead of seventy-three.

A week before Christmas Samuel Bertram's only daughter, Ella, wrote this letter to each of her brothers:

It has occurred to me that it might be an excellent idea if we would plan to spend a little more time this year with Father and Mother when we go for our usual Christmas visit; and what kind of a scheme do you think it would be for us to take the children, and make a real family reunion of it?

I figure that we could all get there by four o'clock the day before Christmas, if we planned for it; and by staying perhaps two days after Christmas we could make quite a visit. What do you say? You see Father and Mother are getting old, and we can't have them with us many more years, anyway; and I'm sure this would please them--only we must be very careful not to make it too exciting for them.

The letters were dispatched with haste, and almost by return mail came the answers; an emphatic approval, and a promise of hearty cooperation signed "Frank" and "Ned."

What is every one's business is apt to be no one's business, however, and no one notified Mr. and Mrs. Samuel Bertram of the change of plan, each thinking that one of the others would attend to it.

"As for presents," mused Ella, as she hurried downtown two days before Christmas, "I never can think what to give them; but, after all, there's nothing better than bed-slippers for Mother, and a warm neckerchief for Father's throat. Those are always good."

The day before Christmas dawned clear and cold. It had been expected that Ella, her husband, and her twin boys would arrive at the little village station a full hour before the train from the north bringing Ned, Mrs. Ned, and little Mabel, together with Frank and his wife and son; but Ella's train was late--so late that it came in a scant five minutes ahead of the other one, and thus brought about a joyous greeting between the reunited families on the station platform itself.

"Why, it's not so bad we were late, after all," cried Ella. "This is fine--now we can all go together!"

"Jove! but we're a cheery sight!" exclaimed Ned, as he counted off on his fingers the blooming faces of those about him. "There are ten of us!"

"Only fancy what they'll say at the house when they catch their first glimpse of us!" chuckled Frank. "The dear old souls! How Father's eyes will shine and Mother's cap-strings bob! By the way, of course they know we're coming to-day?"

There was a moment's silence; then Ella flushed. "Why! didn't--didn't you tell them?" she stammered.

"I? Why, of course not!" cried Frank. "I supposed you were going to. But maybe Ned-" He paused and turned questioning eyes on his brother.

Ned shook his head. "Not I," he said.

"Why, then--then they don't know," cried Ella, aghast. "They don't know a thing!"

"Never mind, come on," laughed Ned. "What difference does it make?"

"'What difference does it make'!" retorted Ella indignantly. "Ned Bertram, do you suppose I'd take the risk of ten of us pouncing down on those two poor dears like this by surprise? Certainly not!"

"But, Ella, they're expecting six of us to-morrow," remonstrated Frank.

"Very true. But that's not ten of us to-day."

"I know; but so far as the work is concerned, you girls always do the most of that," cut in Ned.

"Work! It isn't the work," almost groaned Ella. "Don't you see, boys? It's the excitement--'twouldn't do for them at all. We must fix it some way. Come, let's go into the waiting-room and talk it up."

It was not until after considerable discussion that their plans were finally made and their line of march decided upon. To advance in the open and take the house by storm was clearly out of the question, though Ned remarked that in all probability the dear old creatures would be dozing before the fire, and would not discover their approach. Still, it would be wiser to be on the safe side; and it was unanimously voted that Frank should go ahead alone and reconnoiter, preparing the way for the rest, who could wait, meanwhile, at the little hotel not far from the house.

The short winter day had drawn almost to a close when Frank turned in at the familiar gate of the Bertram homestead. His hand had not reached the white knob of the bell, however, when the eager expectancy of his face gave way to incredulous amazement; from within, clear and distinct, had come the sound of a violin.

"Why, what--" he cried under his breath, and softly pushed open the door.

The hall was almost dark, but the room beyond was a blaze of light, with the curtains drawn, and apparently every lamp the house contained trimmed and burning. He himself stood in the shadow, and his entrance had been unnoticed, though almost the entire expanse of the room before him was visible through the half-open doorway.

In the farther corner of the room a large evergreen tree, sparkling with candles and tinsel stars, was hung with bags of pink and white tarletan and festoons of puffy popcorn. Near it sat an old man playing the violin; and his whole wiry self seemed to quiver with joy to the tune of his merry "Money Musk." In the center of the room two gray-haired men were dancing an old-time jig, bobbing, bowing, and twisting about in a gleeful attempt to outdo each other. Watching them were three old women and another old man, eating ice cream and contentedly munching peppermints. And here, there, and everywhere was the mistress of the house, Lydia Ann herself, cheeks flushed and cap-strings flying, but plainly in her element and joyously content.

For a time the man by the hall door watched in silent amazement; then with a low ejaculation he softly let himself out of the house, and hurried back to the hotel.

"Well?" greeted half a dozen voices; and one added: "What did they say?"

Frank shook his head and dropped into the nearest chair. "I--I didn't tell them," he stammered faintly.

"Didn't tell them!" exclaimed Ella. "Why, Frank, what was the trouble? Were they sick? Surely, they were not upset by just seeing you!" Frank's eyes twinkled "Well, hardly!" he retorted. "They--they're having a party."

"A party!" shrieked half a dozen voices.

"Yes; and a tree, and a dance, and ice cream, and pink peppermints," Frank enumerated in one breath.

There was a chorus of expostulation; then Ella's voice rose dominant. "Frank Bertram, what on earth do you mean?" she demanded. "Who is having all this?"

"Father and Mother," returned Frank, his lips twitching a little. "And they've got old Uncle Tim and half a dozen others for guests."

"But, Frank, how can they be having all this?" faltered Ella. "Why, Father's not so very far from eighty years old, and--Mabel, Mabel, my dear!" she broke off in sudden reproof to her young niece, who had come under her glance at that moment. "Those are presents for Grandpa and Grandma. I wouldn't play with them."

Mabel hesitated, plainly rebellious. In each hand was a gray worsted bed-slipper; atop of her yellow curls was a brown neckerchief, cap fashion.

There were exclamations from two men, and Ned came forward hurriedly. "Oh, I say, Ella," he remonstrated, "you didn't get those for presents, did you?"

"But I did. Why not?" questioned Ella.

"Why, I got slippers, you see. I never can think of anything else. Besides, they're always good, anyhow. But I should think you, a woman, could think of something--"

"Never mind," interrupted Ella airily. "Mother's a dear, and she won't care if she does get two pairs."

"But she won't want three pairs," groaned Frank; "and I got slippers too!"

There was a moment of dismayed silence, then everybody laughed.

Ella was the first to speak. "It's too bad, of course, but never mind. Mother'll see the joke of it just as we do. You know she never seems to care what we give her. Old people don't have many wants, I fancy."

Frank stirred suddenly and walked the length of the room. Then he wheeled about.

"Do you know," he said, a little unsteadily, "I believe that's a mistake?"

"A mistake? What's a mistake?"

"The notion that old people don't have any--wants. See here. They're having a party down there--a party, and they must have got it up themselves. Such being the case, of course they had what they wanted for entertainment--and they aren't drinking tea or knitting socks. They're dancing jigs and eating pink peppermints and ice cream! Their eyes are like stars, and Mother's cheeks are like a girl's; and if you think I'm going to offer those spry young things a brown neckerchief and a pair of bed-slippers you're much mistaken--because I'm not!"

"But what--can--we do?" stammered Ella.

"We can buy something else here--to-night--in the village," declared Frank; "and to-morrow morning we can go and give it to them."

"But--buy what?"

"I haven't the least idea," retorted Frank, with an airy wave of his hands. "Maybe 'twill be a diamond tiara and a polo pony. Anyway, I know what 'twon't be--'twon't be slippers or a neckerchief!"

It was later than usual that Christmas morning when Mr. and Mrs. Samuel Bertram arose. If the old stomachs had rebelled a little at the pink peppermints and ice cream, and if the old feet had charged toll for their unaccustomed activity of the night before, neither Samuel nor Lydia Ann would acknowledge it.

"Well, we had it--that tree!" chuckled Samuel, as he somewhat stiffly thrust himself into his clothes.

"We did, Samuel,--we did," quavered Lydia Ann joyfully, "an' wa'n't it nice? Mis' Hopkins said she never had such a good time in all her life before."

"An' Uncle Tim an' Grandpa Gowin'--they was as spry as crickets, an' they made old Pete tune up that 'Money Musk' three times 'fore they'd quit."

"Yes; an'--my grief an' conscience, Samuel! 'tis late, ain't it?" broke off Lydia Ann, anxiously peering at the clock. "Come, come, dear, you'll have ter hurry 'bout gettin' that tree out of the front room 'fore the children get here. I wouldn't have 'em know for the world how silly we've been--not for the world!"

Samuel bridled, but his movements showed a perceptible increase of speed.

"Well, I do' know," he chuckled.

"'T wa'n't anythin' so awful, after all. But, say," he called triumphantly a moment later, as he stooped and picked up a small object from the floor, "they will find out if you don't hide these 'ere pep'mints!"

The tree and the peppermints had scarcely disappeared from the "front room" when Frank arrived.

"Oh, they're all coming in a minute," he laughed gayly in response to the surprised questions that greeted him. "And we've brought the children, too. You'll have a houseful, all right!"

A houseful it certainly proved to be, and a lively one, too. In the kitchen "the girls" as usual reigned supreme, and bundled off the little mother to "visit with the boys and the children" during the process of dinner-getting, and after dinner they all gathered around the fireplace for games and stories.

"And now," said Frank when darkness came and the lamps were lighted, "I've got a new game, but it's a very mysterious game, and you, Father and Mother, must not know a thing about it until it's all ready." And forthwith he conducted the little old man and the little old woman out into the kitchen with great ceremony.

"Say, Samuel, seems as if this was 'most as good as the party," whispered Lydia Ann excitedly, as they waited in the dark. "I know it; an' they hain't asked us once if we was gettin' too tired! Did ye notice, Lyddy Ann?"

"Yes, an' they didn't make us take naps, either. Ain't it nice? Why, Samuel, I--I shan't mind even the bed-slippers now," she laughed.

"Ready!" called Frank, and the dining-room door was thrown wide open.

The old eyes blinked a little at the sudden light, then widened in amazement. Before the fireplace was a low sewing-table with a chair at each end. The table itself was covered with a white cloth which lay in fascinating little ridges and hillocks indicating concealed treasures beneath. About the table were grouped the four eager-eyed grandchildren and their no less eager-eyed parents. With still another ceremonious bow Frank escorted the little old man and the little old woman to the waiting chairs, and with a merry "One, two, three!" whisked off the cloth.

For one amazed instant there was absolute silence; then Lydia Ann drew a long breath.

"Samuel, Samuel, they're presents--an' for us!" she quavered joyously. "It's the bed-slippers and the neckerchiefs, an' they did 'em all up in white paper an' red ribbons just for us."

At the corner of the mantelpiece a woman choked suddenly and felt for her handkerchief. Behind her two men turned sharply and walked toward the window; but the little old man and the little old woman did not notice it. They had forgotten everything but the enchanting array of mysteries before them.

Trembling old hands hovered over the many-sized, many-shaped packages, and gently patted the perky red bows; but not until the grandchildren impatiently demanded, "Why don't you look at 'em?" did they venture to untie a single ribbon. Then the old eyes shone, indeed, at sight of the wonderful things disclosed; a fine lace tie and a bottle of perfume; a reading-glass and a basket of figs; some dates, raisins, nuts, and candies, and a little electric pocket lantern which would, at the pressure of a thumb, bring to light all the secrets of the darkest of rooms. There were books, too, such as Ella and Frank themselves liked to read; and there was a handsome little clock for the mantel--but there was not anywhere a pair of bed-slippers or a neckerchief.

At last they were all opened, and there remained not one little red bow to untie. On the table, in all their pristine glory, lay the presents, and half-buried in bits of paper and red ribbon sat the amazed, but blissfully happy, little old man and little old woman. Lydia Ann's lips parted, but the trembling words of thanks froze on her tongue--her eyes had fallen on a small pink peppermint on the floor.

"No, no, we can't take 'em," she cried agitatedly. "We hadn't ought to. We was wicked and ongrateful, and last night we--we--" She paused helplessly, her eyes on her husband's face. "Samuel, you--you tell," she faltered.

Samuel cleared his throat.

"Well, ye see, we--yes, last night, we--we--" He could say no more.

"We--we had a party to--to make up for things," blurted out Lydia Ann. "And so ye see we--we hadn't ought ter take these--all these!"

Frank winced. His face grew a little white as he threw a quick glance into his sister's eyes; but his voice, when he spoke, was clear and strong from sheer force of will.

"A party? Good! I'm glad of it. Did you enjoy it?" he asked.

Samuel's jaw dropped. Lydia Ann stared speechlessly. This cordial approval of their folly was more incomprehensible than had been the failure to relegate them to naps and knitting earlier in the afternoon.

"And you've got another party to-night, too; haven't you?" went on Frank smoothly. "As for those things there"--he waved his hand toward the table--"of course you'll take them. Why, we picked them out on purpose for you,--every single one of them,--and only think how we'd feel if you didn't take them! Don't you--like them?"

"'Like them'!" cried Lydia Ann, and at the stifled sob in her voice three men and three women caught their breath sharply and tried to swallow the lumps in their throats. "We--we just love them!"

No one spoke. The grandchildren stared silently, a little awed. Ella, Frank, and Ned stirred restlessly and looked anywhere but at each other.

Lydia Ann flushed, then paled. "Of course, if--if you picked 'em out 'specially for us--" she began hesitatingly, her eyes anxiously scanning the perturbed faces of her children.

"We did--especially," came the prompt reply.

Lydia Ann's gaze drifted to the table and lingered upon the clock, the tie, and the bottle of perfume. "'Specially for us," she murmured softly. Then her face suddenly cleared. "Why, then we'll have to take them, won't we?" she cried, her voice tremulous with ecstasy. "We'll just have to--whether we ought to or not!"

"You certainly will!" declared Frank. And this time he did not even try to hide the shake in his voice.

"Oh!" breathed Lydia Ann blissfully. "Samuel, I--I think I'll take a fig, please!"

Jupiter Ann

It was only after serious consideration that Miss Prue had bought the little horse, Jupiter, and then she changed the name at once. For a respectable spinster to drive any sort of horse was bad enough in Miss Prue's opinion; but to drive a heathen one! To replace "Jupiter" she considered "Ann" a sensible, dignified, and proper name, and "Ann" she named him, regardless of age, sex, or "previous condition of servitude." The villagers accepted the change--though with modifications; the horse was known thereafter as "Miss Prue's Jupiter Ann."

Miss Prue had said that she wanted a safe, steady horse; one that would not run, balk, or kick. She would not have bought any horse, indeed, had it not been that the way to the post office, the store, the church, and everywhere else, had grown so unaccountably long--Miss Prue was approaching her sixtieth birthday. The horse had been hers now a month, and thus far it had been everything that a dignified, somewhat timid spinster could wish it to be. Fortunately--or unfortunately, as one may choose to look at it--Miss Prue did not know that in the dim recesses of Jupiter's memory there lurked the smell of the turf, the feel of the jockey's coaxing touch, and the sound of a triumphant multitude shouting his name; in Miss Prue's estimation the next deadly sin to treason and murder was horse racing.

There was no one in the town, perhaps, who did not know of Miss Prue's abhorrence of horse racing. On all occasions she freed her mind concerning it; and there was a report that the only lover of her youth had lost his suit through his passion for driving fast horses. Even the county fair Miss Prue had refused all her life to attend--there was the horse racing. It was because of all this that she had been so loath to buy a horse, if only the way to everywhere had not grown so long!

For four weeks--indeed, for five--the new horse, Ann, was a treasure; then, one day, Jupiter remembered.

Miss Prue was driving home from the post office. The wide, smooth road led straight ahead under an arch of flaming gold and scarlet. The October air was crisp and bracing, and unconsciously Miss Prue lifted her chin and drew a long breath. Almost at once, however, she frowned. From behind her had come the sound of a horse's hoofs, and reluctantly Miss Prue pulled the right-hand rein.

Jupiter Ann quickened his gait perceptibly, and lifted his head. His ears came erect.

"Whoa, Ann, whoa!" stammered Miss Prue nervously.

The hoof beats were almost abreast now, and hurriedly Miss Prue turned her head. At once she gave the reins an angry jerk; in the other light carriage sat Rupert Joyce, the young man who for weeks had been unsuccessfully trying to find favor in her eyes because he had already found it in the eyes of her ward and niece, Mary Belle.

"Good-morning, Miss Prue," called a boyish voice.

"Good-morning," snapped the woman, and jerked the reins again.

Miss Prue awoke then to the sudden realization that if the other's speed had accelerated, so, too, had her own.

"Ann, Ann, whoa!" she commanded. Then she turned angry eyes on the young man. "Go by--go by! Why don't you go by?" she called sharply.

In obedience, young Joyce touched the whip to his gray mare: but he did not go by. With a curious little shake, as if casting off years of dull propriety, Jupiter Ann thrust forward his nose and got down to business.

Miss Prue grew white, then red. Her hands shook on the reins.

"Ann, Ann, whoa! You mustn't--you can't! Ann, please whoa!" she supplicated wildly. She might as well have besought the wind not to blow.

On and on, neck and neck, the horses raced. Miss Prue's bonnet slipped and hung rakishly above one ear. Her hair loosened and fell in straggling wisps of gray to her shoulders. Her eyeglasses dropped from her nose and swayed dizzily on their slender chain. Her gloves split across the back and showed the white, tense knuckles. Her breath came in gasps, and only a moaning "whoa--whoa" fell in jerky rhythm from her white lips. Ashamed, frightened, and dismayed, Miss Prue clung to the reins and kept her straining eyes on the road ahead.

On and on down the long straight road flew Jupiter Ann and the little gray mare. At door and window of the scudding houses appeared men and women with startled faces and upraised hands. Miss Prue knew that they were there, and shuddered. The shame of it--she, in a horse-race, and with Rupert Joyce! Hurriedly she threw a look at the young man's face to catch its expression; and then she saw something else: the little gray mare was a full half-head in the lead of Jupiter Ann!

It was then that a strange something awoke in Miss Prue--a fierce new something that she had never felt before. Her lips set hard, and her eyes flashed a sudden fire. Her moaning "whoa--whoa" fell silent, and her hands loosened instinctively on the reins. She was leaning forward now, eagerly, anxiously, her eyes on the head of the other horse. Suddenly her tense muscles relaxed, and a look that was perilously near to triumphant joy crossed her face--Jupiter Ann was ahead once more!

By the time the wide sweep of the driveway leading to Miss Prue's home was reached, there was no question of the result, and well in the lead of the little gray mare Jupiter Ann trotted proudly up the driveway and came to a panting stop.

Flushed, disheveled, and palpitating, Miss Prue picked her way to the ground. Behind her Rupert Joyce was just driving into the yard. He, too, was flushed and palpitating--though not for the same reason.

"I--I just thought I'd drive out and see Mary Belle," he blurted out airily, assuming a bold front to meet the wrath which he felt was sure to come. At once, however, his jaw dropped in amazement.

"Mary Belle? I left her down in the orchard gathering apples," Miss Prue was saying cheerfully. "You might look for her there." And she smiled-- the gracious smile of the victor for the vanquished.

Incredulously the youth stared; then, emboldened, he plunged on recklessly:

"I say, you know, Miss Prue, that little horse of yours can run!"

Miss Prue stiffened. With a jerk she straightened her bonnet and thrust her glasses on her nose.

"Ann has been bad--very bad," she said severely. "We'll not talk of it, if you please. I am ashamed of her!" And he turned haughtily away.

And yet--

In the barn two minutes later, Miss Prue patted Jupiter Ann on the neck--a thing she had never done before.

"We beat 'em, anyhow, Ann," she whispered. "And, after all, he's a pleasant-spoken chap, and if Mary Belle wants him--why--let's let her have him!"

The Axminster Path

"There, dear, here we are, all dressed for the day!" said the girl gayly, as she led the frail little woman along the strip of Axminster carpet that led to the big chair.

"And Kathie?" asked the woman, turning her head with the groping uncertainty of the blind.

"Here, mother," answered a cheery voice. "I'm right here by the window."

"Oh!" And the woman smiled happily. "Painting, I suppose, as usual."

"Oh, I'm working, as usual," returned the same cheery voice, its owner changing the position of the garment in her lap and reaching for a spool of silk.

"There!" breathed the blind woman, as she sank into the great chair. "Now I am all ready for my breakfast. Tell cook, please, Margaret, that I will have tea this morning, and just a roll besides my orange." And she smoothed the folds of her black silk gown and picked daintily at the lace in her sleeves.

"Very well, dearie," returned her daughter. "You shall have it right away," she added over her shoulder as she left the room.

In the tiny kitchen beyond the sitting-room Margaret Whitmore lighted the gas-stove and set the water on to boil. Then she arranged a small tray with a bit of worn damask and the only cup and saucer of delicate china that the shelves contained. Some minutes later she went back to her mother, tray in hand.

"'Most starved to death?" she demanded merrily, as she set the tray upon the table Katherine had made ready before the blind woman. "You have your roll, your tea, your orange, as you ordered, dear, and just a bit of currant jelly besides."

"Currant jelly? Well, I don't know,--perhaps it will taste good. 'T was so like Nora to send it up; she's always trying to tempt my appetite, you know. Dear me, girls, I wonder if you realize what a treasure we have in that cook!"

"Yes, dear, I know," murmured Margaret hastily. "And now the tea, Mother--it's getting colder every minute. Will you have the orange first?"

The slender hands of the blind woman hovered for a moment over the table, then dropped slowly and found by touch the position of spoons, plates, and the cup of tea.

"Yes, I have everything. I don't need you any longer, Meg. I don't like to take so much of your time, dear--you should let Betty do for me."

"But I want to do it," laughed Margaret. "Don't you want me?"

"Want you! That isn't the question, dear," objected Mrs. Whitmore gently. "Of course, a maid's service can't be compared for an instant with a daughter's love and care; but I don't want to be selfish--and you and Kathie never let Betty do a thing for me. There, there! I won't scold any more. What are you going to do to-day, Meg?"

Margaret hesitated. She was sitting by the window now, in a low chair near her sister's. In her hands was a garment similar to that upon which Katherine was still at work.

"Why, I thought," she began slowly, "I'd stay here with you and Katherine a while."

Mrs. Whitmore set down her empty cup and turned a troubled face toward the sound of her daughter's voice.

"Meg, dear," she remonstrated, "is it that fancy-work?"

"Well, isn't fancy-work all right?" The girl's voice shook a little.

Mrs. Whitmore stirred uneasily.

"No, it--it isn't--in this case," she protested. "Meg, Kathie, I don't like it. You are young; you should go out more--both of you. I understand, of course; it's your unselfishness. You stay with me lest I get lonely; and you play at painting and fancy-work for an excuse. Now, dearies, there must be a change. You must go out. You must take your place in society. I will not have you waste your young lives."

"Mother!" Margaret was on her feet, and Katherine had dropped her work. "Mother!" they cried again.

"I--I shan't even listen," faltered Margaret. "I shall go and leave you right away," she finished tremulously, picking up the tray and hurrying from the room.

It was hours later, after the little woman had trailed once more along the Axminster path to the bed in the room beyond and had dropped asleep, that Margaret Whitmore faced her sister with despairing eyes.

"Katherine, what shall we do? This thing is killing me!"

The elder girl's lips tightened. For an instant she paused in her work-- but for only an instant.

"I know," she said feverishly; "but we mustn't give up--we mustn't!"

"But how can we help it? It grows worse and worse. She wants us to go out--to sing, dance, and make merry as we used to."

"Then we'll go out and--tell her we dance."

"But there's the work."

"We'll take it with us. We can't both leave at once, of course, but old Mrs. Austin, downstairs, will be glad to have one or the other of us sit with her an occasional afternoon or evening."

Margaret sprang to her feet and walked twice the length of the room.

"But I've--lied so much already!" she moaned, pausing before her sister. "It's all a lie-- my whole life!"

"Yes, yes, I know," murmured the other, with a hurried glance toward the bedroom door. "But, Meg, we mustn't give up--'twould kill her to know now. And, after all, it's only a little while!--such a little while!"

Her voice broke with a half-stifled sob. The younger girl shivered, but did not speak. She walked again the length of the room and back; then she sat down to her work, her lips a tense line of determination, and her thoughts delving into the few past years for a strength that might help her to bear the burden of the days to come.

Ten years before, and one week after James Whitmore's death, Mrs. James Whitmore had been thrown from her carriage, striking on her head and back.

When she came to consciousness, hours afterward, she opened her eyes on midnight darkness, though the room was flooded with sunlight. The optic nerve had been injured, the doctor said. It was doubtful if she would ever be able to see again.

Nor was this all. There were breaks and bruises, and a bad injury to the spine. It was doubtful if she would ever walk again. To the little woman lying back on the pillow it seemed a living death--this thing that had come to her.

It was then that Margaret and Katherine constituted themselves a veritable wall of defense between their mother and the world. Nothing that was not inspected and approved by one or the other was allowed to pass Mrs. Whitmore's chamber door.

For young women only seventeen and nineteen, whose greatest responsibility hitherto had been the selection of a gown or a ribbon, this was a new experience.

At first the question of expense did not enter into consideration. Accustomed all their lives to luxury, they unhesitatingly demanded it now; and doctors, nurses, wines, fruits, flowers, and delicacies were summoned as a matter of course.

Then came the crash. The estate of the supposedly rich James Whitmore was found to be deeply involved, and in the end there was only a pittance for the widow and her two daughters.

Mrs. Whitmore was not told of this at once. She was so ill and helpless that a more convenient season was awaited. That was nearly ten years ago--and she had not been told yet.

Concealment had not been difficult at first. The girls had, indeed, drifted into the deception almost unconsciously, as it certainly was not necessary to burden the ears of the already sorely afflicted woman with the petty details of the economy and retrenchment on the other side of her door.

If her own luxuries grew fewer, the change was so gradual that the invalid did not notice it, and always her blindness made easy the deception of those about her.

Even the move to another home was accomplished without her realizing it--she was taken to the hospital for a month's treatment, and when the month was ended she was tenderly carried home and laid on her own bed; and she did not know that "home" now was a cheap little flat in Harlem instead of the luxurious house on the avenue where her children were born.

She was too ill to receive visitors, and was therefore all the more dependent on her daughters for entertainment.

She pitied them openly for the grief and care she had brought upon them, and in the next breath congratulated them and herself that at least they had all that money could do to smooth the difficult way. In the face of this, it naturally did not grow any easier for the girls to tell the truth--and they kept silent.

For six years Mrs. Whitmore did not step; then her limbs and back grew stronger, and she began to sit up, and to stand for a moment on her feet. Her daughters now bought the strip of Axminster carpet and laid a path across the bedroom, and another one from the bedroom door to the great chair in the sitting-room, so that her feet might not note the straw matting on the floor and question its being there.

In her own sitting-room at home--which had opened, like this, out of her bedroom--the rugs were soft and the chairs sumptuous with springs and satin damask. One such chair had been saved from the wreck--the one at the end of the strip of carpet.

Day by day and month by month the years passed. The frail little woman walked the Axminster path and sat in the tufted chair. For her there were a china cup and plate, and a cook and maids below to serve. For her the endless sewing over which Katherine and Margaret bent their backs to eke out their scanty income was a picture or a bit of embroidery, designed to while away the time.

As Margaret thought of it it seemed incredible--this tissue of fabrications that enmeshed them; but even as she wondered she knew that the very years that marked its gradual growth made now its strength.

And in a little while would come the end--a very little while, the doctor said.

Margaret tightened her lips and echoed her sister's words: "We mustn't give up--we mustn't!"

Two days later the doctor called. He was a bit out of the old life.

His home, too, had been--and was now, for that matter--on the avenue. He lived with his aunt, whose heir he was, and he was the only one outside of the Whitmore family that knew the house of illusions in which Mrs. Whitmore lived.

His visits to the little Harlem flat had long ceased to have more than a semblance of being professional, and it was an open secret that he wished to make Margaret his wife. Margaret said no, though with a heightened color and a quickened breath--which told at least herself how easily the "no" might have been a "yes."

Dr. Littlejohn was young and poor, and he had only his profession, for all he was heir to one of the richest women on the avenue; and Margaret refused to burden him with what she knew it would mean to marry her. In spite of argument, therefore, and a pair of earnest brown eyes that pleaded even more powerfully, she held to her convictions and continued to say no.

All this, however, did not prevent Dr. Littlejohn from making frequent visits to the Whitmore home, and always his coming meant joy to three weary, troubled hearts. To-day he brought a great handful of pink carnations and dropped them into the lap of the blind woman.

"Sweets to the sweet!" he cried gayly, as he patted the slim hand on the arm of the chair.

"Doctor Ned--you dear boy! Oh, how lovely!" exclaimed Mrs. Whitmore, burying her face in the fragrant flowers. "And, doctor, I want to speak to you," she broke off earnestly. "I want you to talk to Meg and Kathie. Perhaps they will listen to you. I want them to go out more. Tell them, please, that I don't need them all the time now."

"Dear me, how independent we are going to be!" laughed the doctor. "And so we don't need any more attention now, eh?"

"Betty will do."

"Betty?" It was hard, sometimes, for the doctor to remember.

"The maid," explained Mrs. Whitmore; "though, for that matter, there might as well be no maid--the girls never let her do a thing for me."

"No?" returned the doctor easily, sure now of where he stood. "But you don't expect me to interfere in this housekeeping business!"

"Somebody must," urged Mrs. Whitmore. "The girls must leave me more. It isn't as if we were poor and couldn't hire nurses and maids. I should die if it were like that, and I were such a burden."

"Mother, dearest!" broke in Margaret feverishly, with an imploring glance toward her sister and the doctor.

"Oh, by the way," interposed the doctor airily, "it has occurred to me that the very object of my visit to-day is right along the lines of what you ask. I want Miss Margaret to go driving with me. I have a call to make out Washington Heights way."

"Oh, but--" began Margaret, and paused at a gesture from her mother.

"There aren't any 'buts' about it," declared Mrs. Whitmore. "Meg shall go."

"Of course she'll go!" echoed Katherine. And with three against her, Margaret's protests were in vain.

Mrs. Whitmore was nervous that night. She could not sleep.

It seemed to her that if she could get up and walk, back and forth, back and forth, she could rest afterward. She had not stepped alone yet, to be sure, since the accident, but, after all, the girls did little more than guide her feet, and she was sure that she could walk alone if she tried.

The more she thought of it the more she longed to test her strength. Just a few steps back and forth, back and forth--then sleep. She was sure she could sleep then. Very quietly, that she might not disturb the sleepers in the bedroom beyond, the blind woman sat up in bed and slipped her feet to the floor.

Within reach were her knit slippers and the heavy shawl always kept at the head of her bed. With trembling hands she put them on and rose upright.

At last she was on her feet, and alone. To a woman who for ten years had depended on others for almost everything but the mere act of breathing, it was joy unspeakable. She stepped once, twice, and again along the side of her bed; then she stopped with a puzzled frown--under her feet was the unyielding, unfamiliar straw matting. She took four more steps, hesitatingly, and with her arms outstretched at full length before her. The next instant she recoiled and caught her breath sharply; her hands had encountered a wall and a window--and there should have been no wall or windows there!

The joy was gone now.

Shaking with fear and weakness, the little woman crept along the wall and felt for something that would tell her that she was still at home. Her feet made no sound, and only her hurried breathing broke the silence.

Through the open door to the sitting-room, and down the wall to the right-on and on she crept.

Here and there a familiar chair or stand met her groping hands and held them hesitatingly for a moment, only to release them to the terror of an unfamiliar corner or window-sill.

The blind woman herself had long since lost all realization of what she was doing. There was only the frenzied longing to find her own. She did not hesitate even at the outer door of the apartment, but turned the key with shaking hands and stepped fearlessly into the hall. The next moment there came a scream and a heavy fall. The Whitmore apartment was just at the head of the stairs, and almost the first step of the blind woman had been off into space.

When Mrs. Whitmore regained consciousness she was alone in her own bed.

Out in the sitting-room, Margaret, Katherine, and the doctor talked together in low tones. At last the girls hurried into the kitchen, and the doctor turned and entered the bedroom. With a low ejaculation he hurried forward.

Mrs. Whitmore flung out her arm and clutched his hand; then she lay back on the pillow and closed her eyes.

"Doctor," she whispered, "where am I?"

"At home, in your own bed." "Where is this place?"

Dr. Littlejohn paled. He sent an anxious glance toward the sitting-room door, though he knew very well that Margaret and Katherine were in the kitchen and could not hear.

"Where is this place?" begged the woman again.

"Why, it--it--is--" The man paused helplessly.

Five thin fingers tightened their clasp on his hand, and the low voice again broke the silence.

"Doctor, did you ever know--did you ever hear that a fall could give back--sight?"

Dr. Littlejohn started and peered into the wan face lying back on the pillow. Its impassiveness reassured him.

"Why, perhaps--once or twice," he returned slowly, falling back into his old position, "though rarely--very rarely."

"But it has happened?"

"Yes, it has happened. There was a case recently in England. The shock and blow released the pressure on the optic nerve; but--"

Something in the face he was watching brought him suddenly forward in his chair. "My dear woman, you don't mean--you can't--"

He did not finish his sentence. Mrs. Whitmore opened her eyes and met his gaze unflinchingly. Then she turned her head.

"Doctor," she said, "that picture on the wall there at the foot of the bed--it doesn't hang quite straight."

"Mrs. Whitmore!" breathed the man incredulously, half rising from his chair.

"Hush! Not yet!" The woman's insistent hand had pulled him back. "Why am I here? Where is this place?"

There was no answer.

"Doctor, you must tell me. I must know."

Again the man hesitated. He noted the flushed cheeks and shaking hands of the woman before him. It was true, she must know; and perhaps, after all, it was best she should know through him. He drew a long breath and plunged straight into the heart of the story.

Five minutes later a glad voice came from the doorway.

"Mother, dearest--then you're awake!" The doctor was conscious of a low-breathed "Hush, don't tell her!" in his ears; then, to his amazement, he saw the woman on the bed turn her head and hold out her hand with the old groping uncertainty of the blind.

"Margaret! It is Margaret, isn't it?"

Days afterward, when the weary, pain-racked body of the little mother was forever at rest, Margaret lifted her head from her lover's shoulder, where she had been sobbing out her grief.

"Ned, I can't be thankful enough," she cried, "that we kept it from Mother to the end. It's my only comfort. She didn't know."

"And I'm sure she would wish that thought to be a comfort to you, dear," said the doctor gently. "I am sure she would."

ACROSS THE YEARS BY ELEANOR H. PORTER

Phineas and the Motor Car

Phineas used to wonder, sometimes, just when it was that he began to court Diantha Bowman, the rosy-cheeked, golden-haired idol of his boyhood. Diantha's cheeks were not rosy now, and her hair was more silver than gold, but she was not yet his wife.

And he had tried so hard to win her! Year after year the rosiest apples from his orchard and the choicest honey from his apiary had found their way to Diantha's table; and year after year the county fair and the village picnic had found him at Diantha's door with his old mare and his buggy, ready to be her devoted slave for the day. Nor was Diantha unmindful of all these attentions. She ate the apples and the honey, and spent long contented hours in the buggy; but she still answered his pleadings with her gentle: "I hain't no call to marry yet, Phineas," and nothing he could do seemed to hasten her decision in the least. It was the mare and the buggy, however, that proved to be responsible for what was the beginning of the end.

They were on their way home from the county fair. The mare, head hanging, was plodding through the dust when around the curve of the road ahead shot the one automobile that the town boasted. The next moment the whizzing thing had passed, and left a superannuated old mare looming through a cloud of dust and dancing on two wabbly hind legs.

"Plague take them autymobiles!" snarled Phineas through set teeth, as he sawed at the reins. "I ax yer pardon, I'm sure, Dianthy," he added shamefacedly, when the mare had dropped to a position more nearly normal; "but I hain't no use fur them 'ere contraptions!"

Diantha frowned. She was frightened--and because she was frightened she was angry. She said the first thing that came into her head--and never had she spoken to Phineas so sharply.

"If you did have some use for 'em, Phineas Hopkins, you wouldn't be crawlin' along in a shiftless old rig like this; you'd have one yourself an' be somebody! For my part, I like 'em, an' I'm jest achin' ter ride in 'em, too!"

Phineas almost dropped the reins in his amazement. "Achin' ter ride in 'em," she had said--and all that he could give her was this "shiftless old rig" that she so scorned. He remembered something else, too, and his face flamed suddenly red. It was Colonel Smith who owned and drove that automobile, and Colonel Smith, too, was a bachelor. What if--Instantly in Phineas's soul rose a fierce jealousy.

"I like a hoss, myself," he said then, with some dignity. "I want somethin' that's alive!"

Diantha laughed slyly. The danger was past, and she could afford to be merry.

"Well, it strikes me that you come pretty near havin' somethin' that wa'n't alive jest 'cause you had somethin' that was!" she retorted. "Really, Phineas, I didn't s'pose Dolly could move so fast!"

Phineas bridled.

"Dolly knew how ter move--once," he rejoined grimly. "'Course nobody pretends ter say she's young now, any more 'n we be," he finished with some defiance. But he drooped visibly at Diantha's next words.

"Why, I don't feel old, Phineas, an' I ain't old, either. Look at Colonel Smith; he's jest my age, an' he's got a autymobile. Mebbe I'll have one some day."

To Phineas it seemed that a cold hand clutched his heart.

"Dianthy, you wouldn't really--ride in one!" he faltered.

Until that moment Diantha had not been sure that she would, but the quaver in Phineas's voice decided her.

"Wouldn't I? You jest wait an' see!"

And Phineas did wait--and he did see. He saw Diantha, not a week later, pink-cheeked and bright-eyed, sitting by the side of Colonel Smith in that hated automobile. Nor did he stop to consider that Diantha was only one of a dozen upon whom Colonel Smith, in the enthusiasm of his new possession, was pleased to bestow that attention. To Phineas it could mean but one thing; and he did not change his opinion when he heard Diantha's account of the ride.

"It was perfectly lovely," she breathed. "Oh, Phineas, it was jest like flyin'!"

"'Flyin'!'" Phineas could say no more. He felt as if he were choking,--choking with the dust raised by Dolly's plodding hoofs.

"An' the trees an' the houses swept by like ghosts," continued Diantha. "Why, Phineas, I could 'a' rode on an' on furever!"

Before the ecstatic rapture in Diantha's face Phineas went down in defeat. Without one word he turned away--but in his heart he registered a solemn vow: he, too, would have an automobile; he, too, would make Diantha wish to ride on and on forever!

Arduous days came then to Phineas. Phineas was not a rich man. He had enough for his modest wants, but until now those wants had not included an automobile--until now he had not known that Diantha wished to fly. All through the autumn and winter Phineas pinched and economized until he had lopped off all of the luxuries and most of the pleasures of living. Even then it is doubtful if he would have accomplished his purpose had he not, in the spring, fallen heir to a modest legacy of a few thousand dollars. The news of his good fortune was not two hours old when he sought Diantha.

"I cal'late mebbe I'll be gettin' me one o' them 'ere autymobiles this spring," he said, as if casually filling a pause in the conversation.

"Phineas!"

At the awed joy in Diantha's voice the man's heart glowed within him. This one moment of triumph was worth all the long miserable winter with its butterless bread and tobaccoless pipes. But he carefully hid his joy when he spoke.

"Yes," he said nonchalantly. "I'm goin' ter Boston next week ter pick one out. I cal'late on gettin' a purty good one."

"Oh, Phineas! But how--how you goin' ter run it?"

Phineas's chin came up.

"Run it!" he scoffed. "Well, I hain't had no trouble yet steerin' a hoss, an' I cal'late I won't have any more steerin' a mess o' senseless metal what hain't got no eyes ter be seein' things an' gittin' scared! I don't worry none 'bout runnin' it."

"But, Phineas, it ain't all steerin'," ventured Diantha, timidly. "There's lots of little handles and things ter turn, an' there's some things you do with your feet. Colonel Smith did."

The name Smith to Phineas was like a match to gunpowder. He flamed instantly into wrath.

"Well, I cal'late what Colonel Smith does, I can," he snapped. "Besides"--airily--"mebbe I shan't git the feet kind, anyhow; I want the best. There's as much as four or five kinds, Jim Blair says, an' I cal'late ter try 'em all."

"Oh-h!" breathed Diantha, falling back in her chair with an ecstatic sigh. "Oh, Phineas, won't it be grand!" And Phineas, seeing the joyous light in her eyes, gazed straight down a vista of happiness that led to wedding bells and bliss.

Phineas was gone some time on his Boston trip. When he returned he looked thin and worried. He started nervously at trivial noises, and his eyes showed a furtive restlessness that quickly caused remark.

"Why, Phineas, you don't look well!" Diantha exclaimed when she saw him.

"Well? Oh, I'm well."

"An' did you buy it--that autymobile?"

"I did." Phineas's voice was triumphant. Diantha's eyes sparkled.

"Where is it?" she demanded.

"Comin'--next week."

"An' did you try 'em all, as you said you would?"

Phineas stirred; then he sighed.

"Well, I dunno," he acknowledged. "I hain't done nothin' but ride in 'em since I went down--I know that. But there's such a powerful lot of 'em, Dianthy; an' when they found out I wanted one, they all took hold an' showed off their best p'ints--'demonstatin','' they called it. They raced me up hill an' down hill, an' scooted me round corners till I didn't know where I was. I didn't have a minute ter myself. An' they went fast, Dianthy--powerful fast. I ain't real sure yet that I'm breathin' natural."

"But it must have been grand, Phineas! I should have loved it!"

"Oh, it was, 'course!" assured Phineas, hastily.

"An' you'll take me ter ride, right away?" If Phineas hesitated it was for only a moment.

"'Course," he promised. "Er--there's a man, he's comin' with it, an' he's goin' ter stay a little, jest ter--ter make sure everything's all right. After he goes I'll come. An' ye want ter be ready--I'll show ye a thing or two!" he finished with a swagger that was meant to hide the shake in his voice.

In due time the man and the automobile arrived, but Diantha did not have her ride at once. It must have taken some time to make sure that "everything was all right," for the man stayed many days, and while he was there, of course Phineas was occupied with him. Colonel Smith was unkind enough to observe that he hoped it was taking Phineas Hopkins long enough to learn to run the thing; but his remark did not reach Diantha's ears. She knew only that Phineas, together with the man and the automobile, started off early every morning for some unfrequented road, and did not return until night.

There came a day, however, when the man left town, and not twenty-four hours later, Phineas, with a gleaming thing of paint and polish, stood at Diantha's door.

"Now ain't that pretty," quavered Diantha excitedly. "Ain't that awful pretty!"

Phineas beamed.

"Purty slick, I think myself," he acknowledged.

"An' green is so much nicer than red," cooed Diantha.

Phineas quite glowed with joy--Colonel Smith's car was red. "Oh, green's the thing," he retorted airily; "an' see!" he added; and forthwith he burst into a paean of praise, in which tires, horns, lamps, pumps, baskets, brakes, and mud-guards were the dominant notes. It almost seemed, indeed, that he had bought the gorgeous thing before him to look at and talk about rather than to use, so loath was he to stop talking and set the wheels to moving. Not until Diantha had twice reminded him that she was longing to ride in it did he help her into the car and make ready to start.

It was not an entire success--that start. There were several false moves on Phineas's part, and Diantha could not repress a slight scream and a nervous jump at sundry unexpected puffs and snorts and snaps from the throbbing thing beneath her. She gave a louder scream when Phineas, in his nervousness, sounded the siren, and a wail like a cry from the spirit world shrieked in her ears.

"Phineas, what was that?" she shivered, when the voice had moaned into silence.

Phineas's lips were dry, and his hands and knees were shaking; but his pride marched boldly to the front.

"Why, that's the siren whistle, 'course," he chattered. "Ain't it great? I thought you'd like it!" And to hear him one would suppose that to sound the siren was always a necessary preliminary to starting the wheels.

They were off at last. There was a slight indecision, to be sure, whether they would go backward or forward, and there was some hesitation as to whether Diantha's geranium bed or the driveway would make the best thoroughfare. But these little matters having been settled to the apparent satisfaction of all concerned, the automobile rolled down the driveway and out on to the main highway.

"Oh, ain't this grand!" murmured Diantha, drawing a long but somewhat tremulous breath.

Phineas did not answer. His lips were tense, and his eyes were fixed on the road ahead. For days now he had run the car himself, and he had been given official assurance that he was quite capable of handling it; yet here he was on his first ride with Diantha almost making a failure of the whole thing at the start. Was he to be beaten--beaten by a senseless motor car and Colonel Smith? At the thought Phineas lifted his chin and put on more power.

"Oh, my! How f-fast we're goin'!" cried Diantha, close to his ear.

Phineas nodded.

"Who wants ter crawl?" he shouted; and the car leaped again at the touch of his hand.

They were out of the town now, on a wide road that had few turns. Occasionally they met a carriage or a wagon, but the frightened horses and the no less frightened drivers gave the automobile a wide berth--which was well; for the parallel tracks behind Phineas showed that the car still had its moments of indecision as to the course to pursue.

The town was four miles behind them when Diantha, who had been for some time vainly clutching at the flying ends of her veil, called to Phineas to stop.

The request took Phineas by surprise. For one awful moment his mind was a blank--he had forgotten how to stop! In frantic haste he turned and twisted and shoved and pulled, ending with so sudden an application of the brakes that Diantha nearly shot head first out of the car as it stopped.

"Why, why--Phineas!" she cried a little sharply.

Phineas swallowed the lump in his throat and steadied himself in his seat.

"Ye see I--I can stop her real quick if I want to," he explained jauntily. "Ye can do 'most anythin' with these 'ere things if ye only know how, Dianthy. Didn't we come slick?"

"Yes, indeed," stammered Diantha, hastily smoothing out the frown on her face and summoning a smile to her lips--not for her best black silk gown would she have had Phineas know that she was wishing herself safe at home and the automobile back where it came from.

"We'll go home through the Holler," said Phineas, after she had retied her veil and they were ready to start. "It's the long way round, ye know. I ain't goin' ter give ye no snippy little two-mile run, Dianthy, like Colonel Smith did," he finished gleefully.

"No, of course not," murmured Diantha, smothering a sigh as the automobile started with a jerk.

An hour later, tired, frightened, a little breathless, but valiantly declaring that she had had a "beautiful time," Diantha was set down at her own door.

That was but the first of many such trips. Ever sounding in Phineas Hopkins's ears and spurring him to fresh endeavor, were Diantha's words, "I could 'a' rode on an' on furever"; and deep in his heart was the determination that if it was automobile rides that she wanted, it was automobile rides that she should have! His small farm on the edge of the town--once the pride of his heart--began to look forlorn and deserted; for Phineas, when not actually driving his automobile, was usually to be found hanging over it with wrench and polishing cloth. He bought little food and less clothing, but always-- gasolene. And he talked to any one who would listen about automobiles in general and his own in particular, learnedly dropping in frequent references to cylinders, speed, horse power, vibrators, carburetors, and spark plugs.

As for Diantha--she went to bed every night with thankfulness that she possessed her complement of limbs and senses, and she rose every morning with a fear that the coming night would find some of them missing. To Phineas and the town in general she appeared to be devoted to this breathless whizzing over the country roads; and wild horses could not have dragged from her the truth: that she was longing with an overwhelming longing for the old days of Dolly, dawdling, and peace.

Just where it all would have ended it is difficult to say had not the automobile itself taken a hand in the game--as automobiles will sometimes--and played trumps.

It was the first day of the county fair again, and Phineas and Diantha were on their way home. Straight ahead the road ran between clumps of green, then unwound in a white ribbon of dust across wide fields and open meadows.

"Tain't much like last year, is it, Dianthy?" crowed Phineas, shrilly, in her ear--then something went wrong.

Phineas knew it instantly. The quivering thing beneath them leaped into new life--but a life of its own. It was no longer a slave, but a master. Phineas's face grew white. Thus far he had been able to keep to the road, but just ahead there was a sharp curve, and he knew he could not make the turn--something was the matter with the steering-gear.

"Look out--she's got the bits in her teeth!" he shouted. "She's bolted!"

There came a scream, a sharp report, and a grinding crash--then silence.

From away off in the dim distance Phineas heard a voice.

"Phineas! Phineas!"

Something snapped, and he seemed to be floating up, up, up, out of the black oblivion of nothingness. He tried to speak, but he knew that he made no sound.

"Phineas! Phineas!"

The voice was nearer now, so near that it seemed just above him. It sounded like--With a mighty effort he opened his eyes; then full consciousness came. He was on the ground, his head in Diantha's lap. Diantha, bonnet crushed, neck-bow askew, and coat torn, was bending over him, calling him frantically by name. Ten feet away the wrecked automobile, tip-tilted against a large maple tree, completed the picture.

With a groan Phineas closed his eyes and turned away his head.

"She's all stove up--an' now you won't ever say yes," he moaned. "You wanted ter ride on an' on furever!"

"But I will--I don't--I didn't mean it," sobbed Diantha incoherently. "I'd rather have Dolly twice over. I like ter crawl. Oh, Phineas, I hate that thing--I've always hated it! I'll say yes next week--to-morrow--to-day if you'll only open your eyes and tell me you ain't a-dyin'!"

Phineas was not dying, and he proved it promptly and effectually, even to the doubting Diantha's blushing content. And there their rescuers found them a long half-hour later-- a blissful old man and a happy old woman sitting hand in hand by the wrecked automobile.

"I cal'lated somebody'd be along purty soon," said Phineas, rising stiffly. "Ye see, we've each got a foot that don't go, so we couldn't git help; but we hain't minded the wait--not a mite!"

ACROSS THE YEARS BY ELEANOR H. PORTER

The Most Wonderful Woman

And a Great Man who proves himself truly great

It was Old Home Week in the little village, and this was to be the biggest day. From a distant city was to come the town's one really Great Man, to speak in the huge tent erected on the Common for just that purpose. From end to end the village was aflame with bunting and astir with excitement, so that even I, merely a weary sojourner in the place, felt the thrill and tingled pleasantly.

When the Honorable Jonas Whitermore entered the tent at two o'clock that afternoon I had a good view of him, for my seat was next the broad aisle. Behind him on the arm of an usher came a small, frightened-looking little woman in a plain brown suit and a plainer brown bonnet set askew above thin gray hair. The materials of both suit and bonnet were manifestly good, but all distinction of line and cut was hopelessly lost in the wearing. Who she was I did not know; but I soon learned, for one of the two young women in front of me said a low something to which the other gave back a swift retort, woefully audible: "His wife? That little dowdy thing in brown? Oh, what a pity! Such an ordinary woman!"

My cheeks grew hot in sympathy with the painful red that swept to the roots of the thin gray hair under the tip-tilted bonnet. Then I glanced at the man.

Had he heard? I was not quite sure. His chin, I fancied, was a trifle higher. I could not see his eyes, but I did see his right hand; and it was clenched so tightly that the knuckles were white with the strain. I thought I knew then. He had heard. The next minute he had passed on up the aisle and the usher was seating the more-frightened-than-ever little wife in the roped-off section reserved for important guests.

It was then that I became aware that the man on my right was saying something.

"I beg your pardon, but-did you speak--to me?" I asked, turning to him hesitatingly.

The old man met my eyes with an abashed smile.

"I guess I'm the party what had ought to be askin' pardon, stranger," he apologized. "I talk to myself so much I kinder furgit sometimes, and do it when folks is round. I was only sayin' that I wondered why 'twas the good Lord give folks tongues and forgot to give 'em brains to run 'em with. But maybe you didn't hear what she said," he hazarded, with a jerk of his thumb toward the young woman in front.

"About Mrs. Whitermore? Yes, I heard."

His face darkened.

"Then you know. And she heard, too! 'Ordinary woman,' indeed! Humph! To think that Betty Tillington should ever live to hear herself called an 'ordinary woman'! You see, I knew her when she was Betty Tillington."

"Did you?" I smiled encouragingly. I was getting interested, and I hoped he would keep on talking. On the platform the guest of honor was holding a miniature reception. He was the picture of polite attention and punctilious responsiveness; but I thought I detected a quick glance now and then toward the roped-off section where sat his wife and I wondered again--had he heard that thoughtless comment?

From somewhere had come the rumor that the man who was to introduce the Honorable Jonas Whitermore had been delayed by a washout "down the road," but was now speeding toward us by automobile. For my part, I fear I wished the absentee a punctured tire so that I might hear more of the heart-history of the faded little woman with the bonnet askew.

"Yes, I knew her," nodded my neighbor, "and she didn't look much then like she does now. She was as pretty as a picture and there wa'n't a chap within sight of her what wa'n't head over heels in love with her. But there wa'n't never a chance for but two of us and we knew it: Joe Whitermore and a chap named Fred Farrell. So, after a time, we just sort of stood off and watched the race--as pretty a race as ever you see. Farrell had the money and the good looks, while Whitermore was poor as a church mouse, and he was homely, too. But Whitermore must have had somethin'--maybe somethin' we didn't see, for she took him.

"Well, they married and settled down happy as two twitterin' birds, but poor as Job's turkey. For a year or so she was as pretty and gay as ever she was and into every good time goin'; then the babies came, one after another, some of 'em livin' and some dyin' soon after they came.

"Of course, things was different then. What with the babies and the housework, Betty couldn't get out much, and we didn't see much of her. When we did see her, though, she'd smile and toss her head in the old way and say how happy she was and didn't we think her babies was the prettiest things ever, and all that. And we did, of course, and told her so.

"But we couldn't help seein' that she was gettin' thin and white and that no matter how she tossed her head, there wa'n't any curls there to bob like they used to, 'cause her hair was pulled straight back and twisted up into a little hard knot just like as if she had done it up when some one was callin' her to come quick."

"Yes, I can imagine it," I nodded.

"Well, that's the way things went at the first, while he was gettin' his start, and I guess they was happy then. You see, they was pullin' even them days and runnin' neck and neck. Even when Fred Farrell, her old beau, married a girl she knew and built a fine house all piazzas and bow-winders right in sight of their shabby little rented cottage, I don't think she minded it; even if Mis' Farrell didn't have anythin' to do from mornin' till night only set in a white dress on her piazza, and rock, and give parties, Betty didn't seem to mind. She had her Joe.

"But by and by she didn't have her Joe. Other folks had him and his business had him. I mean, he'd got up where the big folks in town begun to take notice of him; and when he wa'n't tendin' to business, he was hobnobbin' with them, so's to bring more business. And--of course she, with her babies and housework, didn't have no time for that.

"Well, next they moved away. When they went they took my oldest girl, Mary, to help Betty; and so we still kept track of 'em. Mary said it was worse than ever in the new place. It was quite a big city and just livin' cost a lot. Mr. Whitermore, of course, had to look decent, out among folks as he was, so he had to be 'tended to first. Then what was left of money and time went to the children. It wa'n't long, too, before the big folks there begun to take notice, and Mr. Whitermore would come home all excited and tell about what was said to him and what fine things he was bein' asked to do. He said 'twas goin' to mean everythin' to his career.

"Then come the folks to call, ladies in fine carriages with dressed-up men to hold the door open and all that; but always, after they'd gone, Mary'd find Betty cryin' somewhere, or else tryin' to fix a bit of old lace or ribbon on to some old dress. Mary said Betty's clo's were awful, then. You see, there wa'n't never any money left for her things. But all this didn't last long, for very soon the fine ladies stopped comin' and Betty just settled down to the children and didn't try to fix her clo's any more.

"But by and by, of course, the money begun to come in--lots of it--and that meant more changes, naturally. They moved into a bigger house, and got two more hired girls and a man, besides Mary. Mr. Whitermore said he didn't want his wife to work so hard now, and that, besides, his position demanded it. He was always talkin' about his position those days, tryin' to get his wife to go callin' and go to parties and take her place as his wife, as he put it.

"And Mary said Betty did try, and try hard. Of course she had nice clo's now, lots of 'em; but somehow they never seemed to look just right. And when she did go to parties, she never knew what to talk about, she told Mary. She didn't know a thing about the books and pictures and the plays and quantities of other things that everybody else seemed to know about; and so she just had to sit still and say nothin'.

"Mary said she could see it plagued her and she wa'n't surprised when, after a time, Betty begun to have headaches and be sick party nights, and beg Mr. Whitermore to go alone--and then cry because he did go alone. You see, she'd got it into her head then that her husband was ashamed of her."

"And was--he?" demanded I.

"I don't know. Mary said she couldn't tell exactly. He seemed worried, sometimes, and quite put out at the way his wife acted about goin' to places. Then, other times, he didn't seem to notice or care if he did have to go alone. It wa'n't that he was unkind to her. It was just that he was so busy lookin' after himself that he forgot all about her. But Betty took it all as bein' ashamed of her, no matter what he did; and for a while she just seemed to pine away under it. They'd moved to Washington by that time and, of course, with him in the President's Cabinet, it was pretty hard for her.

"Then, all of a sudden, she took a new turn and begun to study and to try to learn things--everything: how to talk and dress and act, besides stuff that was just book-learnin'. She's been doin' that for quite a spell and Mary says she thinks she'd do pretty well now, in lots of ways, if only she had half a chance--somethin' to encourage her, you know. But her husband don't seem to take no notice, now, just as if he's got tired expectin' anythin' of her and that's made her so scared and discouraged she's too nervous to act as if she did know anythin'. An' there 't is.

"Well, maybe she is just an ordinary woman," sighed the old man, a little sternly, "if bein' 'ordinary' means she's like lots of others. For I suspect, stranger, that, if the truth was told, lots of other big men have got wives just like her--women what have been workin' so tarnal hard to help their husbands get ahead that they hain't had time to see where they themselves was goin'. And by and by they wake up to the fact that they hain't got nowhere. They've just stayed still, 'way behind.

"Mary says she don't believe Betty would mind even that, if her husband only seemed to care--to--to understand, you know, how it had been with her and how--Crickey! I guess they've come," broke off the old man suddenly, craning his neck for a better view of the door.

From outside had sounded the honk of an automobile horn and the wild cheering of men and boys. A few minutes later the long-delayed programme began.

It was the usual thing. Before the Speaker of the Day came other speakers, and each of them, no matter what his subject, failed not to refer to "our illustrious fellow townsman" in terms of highest eulogy. One told of his humble birth, his poverty-driven boyhood, his strenuous youth. Another drew a vivid picture of his rise to fame. A third dilated upon the extraordinary qualities of brain and body which had made such achievement possible and which would one day land him in the White House itself.

Meanwhile, close to the speaker's stand sat the Honorable Jonas Whitermore himself, for the most part grim and motionless, though I thought I detected once or twice a repetition of the half-troubled, half-questioning glances directed toward his wife that I had seen before. Perhaps it was because I was watching him so closely that I saw the sudden change come to his face. The lips lost their perfunctory smile and settled into determined lines. The eyes, under their shaggy brows, glowed with sudden fire. The entire pose and air of the man became curiously alert, as if with the eager impatience of one who has determined upon a certain course of action and is anxious only to be up and doing. Very soon after that he was introduced, and, amid deafening cheers, rose to his feet. Then, very quietly, he began to speak.

We had heard he was an orator. Doubtless many of us were familiar with his famous nickname "Silver-tongued Joe." We had expected great things of him--a brilliant discourse on the tariff, perhaps, or on our foreign relations, or yet on the Hague Tribunal. But we got none of these. We got first a few quiet words of thanks and appreciation for the welcome extended him; then we got the picture of an everyday home just like ours, with all its petty cares and joys so vividly drawn that we thought we were seeing it, not hearing about it. He told us it was a little home of forty years ago, and we began to realize, some way, that he was speaking of himself.

"I may, you know, here," he said, "for I am among my own people. I am at home."

Even then I didn't see what he was coming to. Like the rest I sat slightly confused, wondering what it all meant. Then, suddenly, into his voice there crept a tense something that made me sit more erect in my seat.

"My indomitable will-power? My superb courage? My stupendous strength of character? My undaunted persistence and marvelous capacity for hard work?" he was saying. "Do you think it's to that I owe what I am? Never! Come back with me to that little home of forty years ago and I'll show you to what and to whom I do owe it. First and foremost I owe it to a woman--no ordinary woman, I want you to understand--but to the most wonderful woman in the world."

I knew then. So did my neighbor, the old man at my side. He jogged my elbow frantically and whispered:--

"He's goin' to--he's goin' to! He's goin' to show her he does care and understand! He did hear that girl. Crickey! But ain't he the cute one to pay her back like that, for what she said?"

The little wife down front did not know--yet, however. I realized that, the minute I looked at her and saw her drawn face and her frightened, staring eyes fixed on her husband up there on the platform--her husband, who was going to tell all these people about some wonderful woman whom even she had never heard of before, but who had been the making of him, it seemed.

"My will-power?" the Honorable Jonas Whitermore was saying then. "Not mine, but the will-power of a woman who did not know the meaning of the word 'fail.' Not my superb courage, but the courage of one who, day in and day out, could work for a victory whose crown was to go, not to herself, but to another. Not my stupendous strength of character, but that of a beautiful young girl who could see youth and beauty and opportunity nod farewell, and yet smile as she saw them go. Not my undaunted persistence, but the persistence of one to whom the goal is always just ahead, but never reached. And last, not my marvelous capacity for hard work, but that of the wife and mother who bends her back each morning to a multitude of tasks and cares that she knows night will only interrupt--not finish."

My eyes were still on the little brown-clad woman down in front, so I saw the change come to her face as her husband talked. I saw the terror give way to puzzled questioning, and that, in turn, become surprise, incredulity, then overwhelming joy as the full meaning came to her that she herself was that most wonderful woman in the world who had been the making of him. I looked then for just a touch of the old frightened, self-consciousness at finding herself thus so conspicuous; but it did not come. The little woman plainly had forgotten us. She was no longer Mrs. Jonas Whitermore among a crowd of strangers listening to a great man's Old-Home-Day speech. She was just a loving, heart-hungry, tired, all-but-discouraged wife hearing for the first time from the lips of her husband that he knew and cared and understood.

"Through storm and sunshine, she was always there at her post, aiding, encouraging, that I might be helped," the Honorable Jonas Whitermore was saying. "Week in and week out she fought poverty, sickness, and disappointments, and all without a murmur, lest her complaints distract me for one precious moment from my work. Even the nights brought her no rest, for while I slept, she stole from cot to cradle and from cradle to crib, covering outflung little legs and arms, cooling parched little throats with water, quieting fretful whimpers and hushing threatening outcries with a low 'Hush, darling, mother's here. Don't cry! You'll wake father--and father must have his sleep.' And father had it-- that sleep, just as he had the best of everything else in the house: food, clothing, care, attention--everything.

"What mattered it if her hands did grow rough and toil-worn? Mine were left white and smooth--for my work. What mattered it if her back and her head and her feet did ache? Mine were left strong and painless--for my work. What mattered her wakefulness if I slept? What mattered her weariness if I was rested? What mattered her disappointments if my aims were accomplished? Nothing!"

The Honorable Jonas Whitermore paused for breath, and I caught mine and held it. It seemed, for a minute, as if everybody all over the house was doing the same thing, too, so absolutely still was it, after that one word--"nothing." They were beginning to understand--a little. I could tell that. They were beginning to see this big thing that was taking place right before their eyes. I glanced at the little woman down in front. The tender glow on her face had grown and deepened and broadened until her whole little brown-clad self seemed transfigured. My own eyes dimmed as I looked. Then, suddenly I became aware that the Honorable Jonas Whitermore was speaking again.

"And not for one year only, nor two, nor ten, has this quintessence of devotion been mine," he was saying, "but for twice ten and then a score more--for forty years. For forty years! Did you ever stop to think how long forty years could be--forty years of striving and straining, of pinching and economizing, of serving and sacrificing? Forty years of just loving somebody else better than yourself, and doing this every day, and every hour of the day for the whole of those long forty years? It isn't easy to love somebody else always better than yourself, you know! It means the giving up of lots of things that you want. You might do it for a day, for a month, for a year even--but for forty years! Yet she has done it--that most wonderful woman. Do you wonder that I say it is to her, and to her alone, under God, that I owe all that I am, all that I hope to be?"

Once more he paused. Then, in a voice that shook a little at the first, but that rang out clear and strong and powerful at the end, he said:

"Ladies, gentlemen, I understand this will close your programme. It will give me great pleasure, therefore, if at the adjournment of this meeting you will allow me to present you to the most wonderful woman in the world--my wife."

I wish I could tell you what happened then. The words--oh, yes, I could tell you in words what happened. For that matter, the reporters at the little stand down in front told it in words, and the press of the whole country blazoned it forth on the front page the next morning. But really to know what happened, you should have heard it and seen it, and felt the tremendous power of it deep in your soul, as we did who did see it.

There was a moment's breathless hush, then to the canvas roof there rose a mighty cheer and a thunderous clapping of hands as by common impulse the entire audience leaped to its feet.

For one moment only did I catch a glimpse of Mrs. Jonas Whitermore, blushing, laughing, and wiping teary eyes in which the wondrous glow still lingered; then the eager crowd swept down the aisle toward her.

"Crickey!" breathed the red-faced old man at my side. "Well, stranger, even if it does seem sometimes as if the good Lord give some folks tongues and forgot to give 'em brains to run 'em with, I guess maybe He kinder makes up for it, once in a while, by givin' other folks the brains to use their tongues so powerful well!"

I nodded dumbly. I could not speak just then--but the young woman in front of me could. Very distinctly as I passed her I heard her say:

"Well, now, ain't that the limit, Sue? And her such an ordinary woman, too!"

ACROSS THE YEARS BY ELEANOR H. PORTER

The Price of a Pair of Shoes

For fifty years the meadow lot had been mowed and the side hill ploughed at the nod of Jeremiah's head; and for the same fifty years the plums had been preserved and the mince-meat chopped at the nod of his wife's-- and now the whole farm from the meadowlot to the mince-meat was to pass into the hands of William, the only son, and William's wife, Sarah Ellen.

"It'll be so much nicer, mother,--no care for you!" Sarah Ellen had declared.

"And so much easier for you, father, too," William had added. "It's time you rested. As for money--of course you'll have plenty in the savings-bank for clothes and such things. You won't need much, anyhow," he finished, "for you'll get your living off the farm just as you always have."

So the matter was settled, and the papers were made out. There was no one to be considered, after all, but themselves, for William was the only living son, and there had been no daughters.

For a time it was delightful. Jeremiah and Hester Whipple were like children let out of school. They told themselves that they were people of leisure now, and they forced themselves to lie abed half an hour later than usual each day. They spent long hours in the attic looking over old treasures, and they loitered about the garden and the barn with no fear that it might be time to get dinner or to feed the stock.

Gradually, however, there came a change. A new restlessness entered their lives, a restlessness that speedily became the worst kind of homesickness--the homesickness of one who is already at home.

The extra half-hour was spent in bed as before--but now Hester lay with one ear listening to make sure that Sarah Ellen did let the cat in for her early breakfast; and Jeremiah lay with his ear listening for the squeak of the barn door which would tell him whether William was early or, late that morning. There were the same long hours in the attic and the garden, too--but in the attic Hester discovered her treasured wax wreath (late of the parlor wall); and in the garden Jeremiah found more weeds than he had ever allowed to grow there, he was sure.

The farm had been in the hands of William and Sarah Ellen just six months when the Huntersville Savings Bank closed its doors. It was the old story of dishonesty and disaster, and when the smoke of Treasurer Hilton's revolver cleared away there was found to be practically nothing for the depositors. Perhaps on no one did the blow fall with more staggering force than on Jeremiah Whipple.

"Why, Hester," he moaned, when he found himself alone with his wife, "here I'm seventy-eight years old--an' no money! What am I goin' ter do?"

"I know, dear," soothed Hester; "but 't ain't as bad for us as 'tis for some. We've got the farm, you know; an'--"

"We hain't got the farm," cut in her husband sharply. "William an' Sarah Ellen's got it."

"Yes, I know, but they--why, they're us, Jeremiah," reminded Hester, trying to keep the quaver out of her voice.

"Mebbe, Hester, mebbe," conceded Jeremiah; but he turned and looked out of the window with gloomy eyes.

There came a letter to the farmhouse soon after this from Nathan Banks, a favorite nephew, suggesting that "uncle and aunt" pay them a little visit.

"Just the thing, father!" cried William. "Go--it'll do you both good!" And after some little talk it was decided that the invitation should be accepted.

Nathan Banks lived thirty miles away, but not until the night before the Whipples were to start did it suddenly occur to Jeremiah that he had now no money for railroad tickets. With a heightened color on his old cheeks he mentioned the fact to William.

"Ye see, I--I s'pose I'll have ter come ter you," he apologized. "Them won't take us!" And he looked ruefully at a few coins he had pulled from his pocket. "They're all the cash I've got left."

William frowned a little and stroked his beard.

"Sure enough!" he muttered. "I forgot the tickets, too, father. 'T is awkward--that bank blowing up; isn't it? Oh, I'll let you have it all right, of course, and glad to, only it so happens that just now I--er, how much is it, anyway?" he broke off abruptly.

"Why, I reckon a couple of dollars'll take us down, an' more, mebbe," stammered the old man, "only, of course, there's comin' back, and--"

"Oh, we don't have to reckon on that part now," interrupted William impatiently, as he thrust his hands into his pockets and brought out a bill and some change. "I can send you down some more when that time comes. There, here's a two; if it doesn't take it all, what's left can go toward bringing you back."

And he handed out the bill, and dropped the change into his pocket.

"Thank you, William," stammered the old man. "I--I'm sorry--"

"Oh, that's all right," cut in William cheerfully, with a wave of his two hands. "Glad to do it, father; glad to do it!"

Mr. and Mrs. Whipple stayed some weeks with their nephew. But, much as they enjoyed their visit, there came a day when home--regardless of weeds that were present and wax wreaths that were absent--seemed to them the one place in the world; and they would have gone there at once had it not been for the railroad fares.

William had not sent down any more money, though his letters had been kind, and had always spoken of the warm welcome that awaited them any time they wished to come home.

Toward the end of the fifth week a bright idea came to Jeremiah.

"We'll go to Cousin Abby's," he announced gleefully to his wife. "Nathan said last night he'd drive us over there any time. We'll go to-morrow, an' we won't come back here at all--it'll be ten miles nearer home there, an' it won't cost us a cent ter get there," he finished triumphantly. And to Cousin Abby's they went.

So elated was Jeremiah with the result of his scheming that he set his wits to work in good earnest, and in less than a week he had formulated an itinerary that embraced the homes of two other cousins, an aunt of Sarah Ellen's, and the niece of a brother-in-law, the latter being only three miles from 'his own farmhouse--or rather William's farmhouse, as he corrected himself bitterly. Before another month had passed, the round of visits was accomplished, and the little old man and the little old woman--having been carried to their destination in each case by their latest host--finally arrived at the farmhouse door. They were weary, penniless, and half-sick from being feasted and fêted at every turn, but they were blissfully conscious that of no one had they been obliged to beg the price of their journey home.

"We didn't write we were comin'," apologized Jeremiah faintly, as he stumbled across the threshold and dropped into the nearest chair. "We were goin' ter write from Keziah's, but we were so tired we hurried right up an' come home. 'Tis nice ter get here; ain't it, Hester?" he finished, settling back in his chair.

"'Nice'!" cried Hester tremulously, tugging at her bonnet strings. "'Nice' ain't no name for it, Jeremiah. Why, Sarah Ellen, seems if I don't want to do nothin' for a whole month but set in my own room an' jest look 'round all day!"

"You poor dear--and that's all you shall do!" soothed Sarah Ellen; and Hester sighed, content. For so many, many weeks now she had sat upon strange chairs and looked out upon an unfamiliar world!

It was midwinter when Jeremiah's last pair of shoes gave out. "An' there ain't a cent ter get any new ones, Hester," he exclaimed, ruefully eying the ominously thin place in the sole.

"I know, Jeremiah, but there's William," murmured Hester. "I'm sure he--"

"Oh, of course, he'd give it to me," cried Jeremiah quickly; "but--I--I sort of hate to ask."

"Pooh! I wouldn't think of that," declared Hester stoutly, but even as she spoke, she tucked her own feet farther under her chair. "We gave them the farm, and they understood they was to take care of us, of course."

"Hm-m, yes, I know, I know. I'll ask him," murmured Jeremiah--but he did not ask him until the ominously thin place in the sole had become a hole, large, round, and unmistakable.

"Well, William," he began jocosely, trying to steady his shaking voice, "guess them won't stand for it much longer!" And he held up the shoe, sole uppermost.

"Well, I should say not!" laughed William; then his face changed. "Oh, and you'll have to have the money for some new ones, of course. By George! It does beat all how I keep forgetting about that bank!"

"I know, William, I'm sorry," stammered the old man miserably.

"Oh, I can let you have it all right, father, and glad to," assured William, still frowning. "It's only that just at this time I'm a little short, and--" He stopped abruptly and thrust his hands into his pockets. "Hm-m," he vouchsafed after a minute. "Well, I'll tell you what--I haven't got any now, but in a day or two I'll take you over to the village and see what Skinner's got that will fit you. Oh, we'll have some shoes, father, never fear!" he laughed. "You don't suppose I'm going to let my father go barefoot!--eh?" And he laughed again.

Things wore out that winter in the most unaccountable fashion--at least those belonging to Jeremiah and Hester did, especially undergarments. One by one they came to mending, and one by one Hester mended them, patch upon patch, until sometimes there was left scarcely a thread of the original garment. Once she asked William for money to buy new ones, but it happened that William was again short, and though the money she had asked for came later, Hester did not make that same request again.

There were two things that Hester could not patch very successfully--her shoes. She fried to patch them to be sure, but the coarse thread knotted in her shaking old hands, and the bits of leather--cut from still older shoes--slipped about and left her poor old thumb exposed to the sharp prick of the needle, so that she finally gave it up in despair. She tucked her feet still farther under her chair these days when Jeremiah was near, and she pieced down two of her dress skirts so that they might touch the floor all round. In spite of all this, however, Jeremiah saw, one day--and understood.

"Hester," he cried sharply, "put out your foot."

Hester did not hear--apparently. She lowered the paper she was reading and laughed a little hysterically.

"Such a good joke, Jeremiah!" she quavered. "Just let me read it. A man--"

"Hester, be them the best shoes you've got?" demanded Jeremiah.

And Hester, with a wisdom born of fifty years' experience of that particular tone of voice, dropped her paper and her subterfuge, and said gently: "Yes, Jeremiah."

There was a moment's pause; then Jeremiah sprang to his feet, thrust his hands into his pockets, and paced the tiny bedroom from end to end.

"Hester, this thing's a-killin' me!" he blurted out at last. "Here I'm seventy-eight years old--an' I hain't got money enough ter buy my wife a pair of shoes!"

"But the farm, Jeremiah--"

"I tell ye the farm ain't mine," cut in Jeremiah savagely. "Look a-here, Hester, how do you s'pose it feels to a man who's paid his own way since he was a boy, bought a farm with his own money an' run it, brought up his boys an' edyercated 'em--how do ye s'pose it feels fur that man ter go ter his own son an' say: 'Please, sir, can't I have a nickel ter buy me a pair o' shoestrings?' How do ye s'pose it feels? I tell ye, Hester, I can't stand it-- I jest can't! I'm goin' ter work."

"Jere-mi-ah!"

"Well, I am," repeated the old man doggedly. "You're goin' ter have some shoes, an' I'm goin' ter earn 'em. See if I don't!" And he squared his shoulders, and straightened his bent back as if already he felt the weight of a welcome burden.

Spring came, and with it long sunny days and the smell of green things growing. Jeremiah began to be absent day after day from the farmhouse. The few tasks that he performed each morning were soon finished, and after that he disappeared, not to return until night. William wondered a little, but said nothing. Other and more important matters filled his mind.

Only Hester noticed that the old man's step grew more languid and his eye more dull; and only Hester knew that at night he was sometimes too tired to sleep--that he could not "seem ter hit the bed," as he expressed it.

It was at about this time that Hester began to make frequent visits to the half-dozen farmhouses in the settlement about them. She began to be wonderfully busy these days, too, knitting socks and mittens, or piecing up quilts. Sarah Ellen asked her sometimes what she was doing, but Hester's answers were always so cheery and bright that Sarah Ellen did not realize that the point was always evaded and the subject changed.

It was in May that the inevitable happened. William came home one day to find an excited, weeping wife who hurried him into the seclusion of their own room.

"William, William," she moaned, "what shall we do? It's father and mother; they've--oh, William, how can I tell you!" and she covered her face with her hands.

William paled under his coat of tan. He gripped his wife's arm with fingers that hurt.

"What is it--what's happened?" he asked hoarsely. "They aren't hurt or--dead?"

"No, no," choked Sarah Ellen. "I didn't mean to frighten you. They're all right that way. They--they've gone to work! William, what shall we do?"

Again William Whipple gripped his wife's arm with fingers that hurt.

"Sarah Ellen, quit that crying, for Heaven's sake! What does this mean? What are you talking about?" he demanded.

Sarah Ellen sopped her eyes with her handkerchief and lifted her head.

"It was this morning. I was over to Maria Weston's," she explained brokenly. "Maria dropped something about a quilt mother was piecing for her, and when I asked her what in the world she meant, she looked queer, and said she supposed I knew. Then she tried to change the subject; but I wouldn't let her, and finally I got the whole story out of her."

"Yes, yes, go on," urged William impatiently, as Sarah Ellen paused for breath.

"It seems mother came to her a while ago, and--and she went to others, too. She asked if there wasn't some knitting or patchwork she could do for them. She said she--she wanted to earn some money." Sarah Ellen's voice broke over the last word, and William muttered something under his breath. "She said they'd lost all they had in the bank," went on Sarah Ellen hurriedly, "and that they didn't like to ask you for money."

"Why, I always let them have--" began William defensively; then he stopped short, a slow red staining his face.

"Yes, I know you have," interposed Sarah Ellen eagerly; "and I said so to Maria. But mother had already told her that, it seems. She said that mother said you were always glad to give it to them when they asked for it, but that it hurt father's pride to beg, so he'd gone to work to earn some of his own."

"Father!" exclaimed William. "But I thought you said 'twas mother. Surely father isn't knitting socks and mittens, is he?"

"No, no," cried Sarah Ellen. "I'm coming to that as fast as I can. You see, 'twas father who went to work first. He's been doing all sorts of little odd jobs, even to staying with the Snow children while their folks went to town, and spading up Nancy Howe's flower beds for her. But it's been wearing on him, and he was getting all tired out. Only think of it, William--working out--father and mother! I just can't ever hold up my head again! What shall we do?"

"Do? Why, we'll stop it, of course," declared William savagely. "I guess I can support my own father and mother without their working for a living!"

"But it's money, William, that they want. Don't you see?"

"Well, we'll give them money, then. I always have, anyway,--when they asked for it," finished William in an aggrieved voice.

Sarah Ellen shook her head.

"It won't do," she sighed. "It might have done once--but not now. They've got to the point where they just can't accept money doled out to them like that. Why, just think, 't was all theirs once!"

"Well, 'tis now--in a way."

"I know--but we haven't acted as if it were. I can see that now, when it's too late."

"We'll give it back, then," cried William, his face clearing; "the whole blamed farm!"

Sarah Ellen frowned. She shook her head slowly, then paused, a dawning question in her eyes.

"You don't suppose--William, could we?" she cried with sudden eagerness.

"Well, we can try mighty hard," retorted the man grimly. "But we've got to go easy, Sarah Ellen,--no bungling. We've got to spin some sort of a yarn that won't break, nor have any weak places; and of course, as far as the real work of the farm is concerned, we'll still do the most of it. But the place'll be theirs. See?--theirs! Working out--good Heavens!"

It must have been a week later that Jeremiah burst into his wife's room. Hester sat by the window, bending over numberless scraps of blue, red, and pink calico.

"Put it up, put it up, Hester," he panted joyously. "Ye hain't got to sew no more, an' I hain't neither. The farm is ours!"

"Why, Jeremiah, what--how--"

"I don't know, Hester, no more than you do," laughed Jeremiah happily; "only William says he's tired of runnin' things all alone, an' he wants me to take hold again. They're goin' ter make out the papers right away; an' say, Hester,"--the bent shoulders drew themselves erect with an air of pride,--"I thought mebbe this afternoon we'd drive over ter Huntersville an' get some shoes for you. Ye know you're always needin' shoes!"

The Long Road

"Jane!"

"Yes, father."

"Is the house locked up?"

"Yes."

"Are ye sure, now?"

"Why, yes, dear; I just did it."

"Well, won't ye see?"

"But I have seen, father." Jane did not often make so many words about this little matter, but she was particularly tired to-night.

The old man fell back wearily.

"Seems ter me, Jane, ye might jest see," he fretted. "'T ain't much I'm askin' of ye, an' ye know them spoons--"

"Yes, yes, dear, I'll go," interrupted the woman hurriedly.

"And, Jane!"

"Yes." The woman turned and waited. She knew quite well what was coming, but it was the very exquisiteness of her patient care that allowed her to give no sign that she had waited in that same spot to hear those same words every night for long years past.

"An' ye might count 'em--them spoons," said the old man.

"Yes."

"An' the forks."

"Yes."

"An' them photygraph pictures in the parlor."

"All right, father." The woman turned away. Her step was slow, but confident--the last word had been said.

To Jane Pendergast her father had gone with the going of his keen, clear mind, twenty years before. This fretful, childish, exacting old man that pottered about the house all day was but the shell that had held the kernel--the casket that had held the jewel. But because of what it had held, Jane guarded it tenderly, laying at its feet her life as a willing sacrifice.

There had been four children: Edgar, the eldest; Jane, Mary, and Fred. Edgar had left home early, and was a successful business man in Boston. Mary had married a wealthy lawyer of the same city; and Fred had opened a real estate office in a thriving Southern town.

Jane had stayed at home. There had been a time, it is true, when she had planned to go away to school; but the death of Mrs. Pendergast left no one at home to care for Mary and Fred, so Jane had abandoned the idea. Later, after Mary had married and Fred had gone away, there was still her father to be cared for, though at this time he was well and strong.

Jane had passed her thirty-fifth birthday, when she became palpitatingly aware of a pair of blue-gray eyes, and a determined, smooth-shaven chin belonging to the recently arrived principal of the village school. In spite of her stern admonition to herself to remember her years and not quite lose her head, she was fast drifting into a rosy dream of romance that was all the more enthralling because so belated, when the summons of a small boy brought her sharply back to the realities.

"It's yer father, miss. They want ye ter come," he panted. "Somethin' has took him. He's in Mackey's drug store, talkin' awful queer. He ain't his self, ye know. They thought maybe you could--do somethin'."

Jane went at once--but she could do nothing except to lead gently home the chattering, shifting-eyed thing that had once been her father. One after another the village physicians shook their heads--they could do nothing. Skilled alienists from the city--they, too, could do nothing. There was nothing that could be done, they said, except to care for him as one would for a child. He would live years, probably. His constitution was wonderfully good. He would not be violent--just foolish and childish, with perhaps a growing irritability as the years passed and his physical strength failed.

Mary and Edgar had come home at once. Mary had stayed two days and Edgar five hours. They were shocked and dismayed at their father's condition. So overwhelmed with grief were they, indeed, that they fled from the room almost immediately upon seeing him, and Edgar took the first train out of town.

Mary, shiveringly, crept from room to room, trying to find a place where the cackling laugh and the fretful voice would not reach her. But the old man, like a child with a new toy, was pleased at his daughter's arrival, and followed her about the house with unfailing persistence.

"But, Mary, he won't hurt you. Why do you run?" remonstrated Jane.

Mary shuddered and covered her face with her hands.

"Jane, Jane, how can you take it so calmly!" she moaned. "How can you bear it?"

There was a moment's pause. A curious expression had come to Jane's face.

"Some one--has to," she said at last, quietly.

Jane went down to the village the next afternoon, leaving her sister in charge at home. When she returned, an hour later, Mary met her at the gate, crying and wringing her hands.

"Jane, Jane, I thought you would never come! I can't do a thing with him. He insists that he isn't at home, and that he wants to go there. I told him, over and over again, that he was at home already, but it didn't do a bit of good. I've had a perfectly awful time."

"Yes, I know. Where is he?"

"In the kitchen. I--I tied him. He just would go, and I couldn't hold him."

"Oh, Mary!" And Jane fairly flew up the walk to the kitchen door. A minute later she appeared, leading an old man, who was whimpering pitifully.

"Home, Jane. I want ter go home."

"Yes, dear, I know. We'll go." And Mary watched with wondering eyes while the two walked down the path, through the gate and across the street to the next corner, then slowly crossed again and came back through the familiar doorway.

"Home!" chuckled the old man gleefully.

"We've come home!"

Mary went back to Boston the next day. She said it was fortunate, indeed, that Jane's nerves were so strong. For her part, she could not have stood it another day.

The days slipped into weeks, and the weeks into months. Jane took the entire care of her father, except that she hired a woman to come in for an hour or two once or twice a week, when she herself was obliged to leave the house.

The owner of the blue-gray eyes did not belie the determination of his chin, but made a valiant effort to establish himself on the basis of the old intimacy; but Miss Pendergast held herself sternly aloof, and refused to listen to him. In a year he had left town--but it was not his fault that he was obliged to go away alone, as Jane Pendergast well knew.

One by one the years passed. Twenty had gone by now since the small boy came with his fateful summons that June day. Jane was fifty-five now, a thin-faced, stoop-shouldered, tired woman--but a woman to whom release from this constant care was soon to come, for she was not yet fifty-six when her father died.

All the children and some of the grandchildren came to the funeral. In the evening the family, with the exception of Jane, gathered in the sitting-room and discussed the future, while upstairs the woman whose fate was most concerned laid herself wearily in bed with almost a pang that she need not now first be doubly sure that doors were locked and spoons were counted.

In the sitting-room below, discussion waxed warm.

"But what shall we do with her?" demanded Mary. "I had meant to give her my share of the property," she added with an air of great generosity, "but it seems there's nothing to give."

"No, there's nothing to give," returned Edgar. "The house had to be mortgaged long ago to pay their living expenses, and it will have to be sold."

"But she's got to live somewhere!" Mary's voice was fretful, questioning.

For a moment there was silence; then Edgar stirrad in his chair.

"Well, why can't she go to you, Mary?" he asked.

"Me!" Mary almost screamed the word.

"Why, Edgar!--when you know how much I have on my hands with my great house and all my social duties, to say nothing of Belle's engagement!"

"Well, maybe Jane could help."

"Help! How, pray?--to entertain my guests?" And even Edgar smiled as he thought of Jane, in her five-year-old bonnet and her ten-year-old black gown, standing in the receiving line at an exclusive Commonwealth Avenue reception.

"Well, but--" Edgar paused impotently.

"Why don't you take her?" It was Mary who made the suggestion.

"I? Oh, but I--" Edgar stopped and glanced uneasily at his wife.

"Why, of course, if it's necessary," murmured Mrs. Edgar, with a resigned air. "I should certainly never wish it said that I refused a home to any of my husband's poor relations."

"Oh, good Heavens! Let her come to us," cut in Fred sharply. "I reckon we can take care of our 'poor relations' for a spell yet; eh, Sally?"

"Why, sure we can," retorted. Fred's wife, in her soft Southern drawl. "We'll be right glad to take her, I reckon." And there the matter ended.

Jane Pendergast had been South two months, when one day Edgar received a letter from his brother Fred.

Jane's going North [wrote Fred]. Sally says she can't have her in the house another week. 'Course, we don't want to tell Jane exactly that-- but we've fixed it so she's going to leave.

I'm sorry if this move causes you folks any trouble, but there just wasn't any other way out of it. You see, Sally is Southern and easy-going, and I suppose not over-particular in the eyes of you stiff Northerners. I don't mind things, either, and I suppose I'm easy, too.

Well, great Scott!--Jane hadn't been down here five minutes before she began to "slick up," as she called it--and she's been "slickin' up" ever since. Sally always left things round handy, and so've the children; but since Jane came, we haven't been able to find a thing when we wanted it. All our boots and shoes are put away, turned toes out, and all our hats and coats are snatched up and hung on pegs the minute we toss them off.

Maybe this don't seem much to you, but it's lots to us. Anyhow, Jane's going North. She says she's going to visit Edgar a little while, and I told her I'd write and tell you she's coming. She'll be there about the 20th. Will wire you what train.

Your affectionate brother

Fred

As gently as possible Edgar broke to his wife the news of the prospective guest. Julia Pendergast was a good woman. At least she often said that she was, adding, at the same time, that she never knowingly refused to do her duty. She said the same thing now to her husband, and she immediately made some very elaborate and very apparent changes in her home and in her plans, all with an eye to the expected guest. At four o'clock Wednesday afternoon Edgar met his sister at the station.

"Well, I don't see as you've changed much," he said kindly.

"Haven't I? Why, seems as if I must look changed a lot," chirruped Jane. "I'm so rested, and Fred and Sally were so good to me! Why, they tried not to have me do a thing--and I didn't do much, only a little puttering around just to help out with the work."

"Hm-m," murmured Edgar. "Well, I'm glad to see you're--rested."

Julia met them in the hall of the beautiful Brookline residence. Lined up with her were the four younger children, who lived at home. They made an imposing array, and Jane was visibly affected.

"Oh, it's so good of you--to meet me--like this!" she faltered.

"Why, we wished to, I'm sure," returned Mrs. Pendergast, with a half-stifled sigh. "I hope I understand my duty to my guest and my sister-in-law sufficiently to know what is her due. I did not allow anything--not even my committee meeting to-day--to interfere with this call for duty at home."

Jane fell back. All the glow fled from her face.

"Oh, then you did stay at home--and for me! I'm so sorry," she stammered.

But Mrs. Pendergast raised a deprecatory hand.

"Say no more. It was nothing. Now come, let me show you to your room. I've given you Ella's room, and put Ella in Tom's, and Tom in Bert's, and moved Bert upstairs to the little room over--"

"Oh, don't!" interrupted Jane, in quick distress. "I don't want to put people out so! Let me go upstairs." Mrs. Pendergast frowned and sighed. She had the air of one whose kindest efforts are misunderstood.

"My dear Jane, I am sorry, but I shall have to ask you to be as satisfied as you can be with the arrangements I am able to make for you. You see, even though this house is large, I am, in a way, cramped for room. I always have to keep three guest-rooms ready for immediate occupancy. I am a member of four clubs and six charitable and religious organizations, besides the church, and there are always ministers and delegates whom I feel it my duty to entertain."

"But that is all the more reason why I should go upstairs, and not put all those children out of their rooms," begged Jane.

Mrs. Pendergast shook her head.

"It does them good," she said decidedly, "to learn to be self-sacrificing. That is a virtue we all must learn to practice."

Jane flushed again; then she turned abruptly. "Julia, did you want me to--to come to see you?" she asked.

"Why, certainly; what a question!" returned Mrs. Pendergast, in a properly shocked tone of voice. "As if I could do otherwise than to want my husband's sister to come to us."

Jane smiled faintly, but her eyes were troubled.

"Thank you; I'm glad you feel--that way. You see, at Fred's--I wouldn't have them know it for the world, they were so good to me--but I thought, lately, that maybe they didn't want--But it wasn't so, of course. It couldn't have been. I--I ought not even to think it."

"Hm-m; no," returned Mrs. Pendergast, with noncommittal briefness.

Not six weeks later Mary, in her beautiful Commonwealth Avenue home, received a call from a little, thin-faced woman, who curtsied to the butler and asked him to please tell her sister that she wished to speak to her.

Mary looked worried and not over-cordial when she rustled into the room.

"Why, Jane, did you find your way here all alone?" she cried.

"Yes--no--well, I asked a man at the last; but, you know, I've been here twice before with the others."

"Yes, I know," said Mary.

There was a pause; then Jane cleared her throat timidly.

"Mary, I--I've been thinking. You see, just as soon as I'm strong enough, I--I'm going to take care of myself, and then I won't be a burden to--to anybody." Jane was talking very fast now. Her words came tremulously between short, broken breaths. "But until I get well enough to earn money, I can't, you see. And I've been thinking;--would you be willing to take me until--until I can? I'm lots better, already, and getting stronger every day. It wouldn't be for--long."

"Why, of course, Jane!" Mary spoke cheerfully, and in a tone a little higher than her ordinary voice. "I should have asked you to come here before, only I feared you wouldn't be happy here--such a different life for you, and so much noise and confusion with Belle's wedding coming on, and all!"

Jane gave her a grateful glance.

"I know, of course,--you'd think that,--and it isn't that I'm finding fault with Julia and Edgar. I couldn't do that--they're so good to me. But, you see, I put them out so. Now, there's my room, for one thing. 'T was Ella's, and Ella has to keep running in for things she's left, and she says it's the same with the others. You see, I've got Ella's room, and Ella's got Tom's, and Tom's got Bert's. It's a regular 'house that Jack built'--and I'm the 'Jack'!"

"I see," laughed Mary constrainedly. "And you want to come here? Well, you shall. You--you may come a week from Saturday," she added, after a pause. "I have a reception and a dinner here the first of the week, and--you'd better stay away until after that."

"Oh, thank you," sighed Jane. "You are so good. I shall tell Julia that I'm invited here, so she won't think I'm dissatisfied. They're so good to me--I wouldn't want to hurt their feelings!"

"Of course not," murmured Mary.

The big, fat tire of the touring-car popped like a pistol shot directly in front of the large white house with the green blinds.

"This is the time we're in luck, Belle," laughed the good-natured young fellow who had been driving the car. "Do you see that big piazza just aching for you to come and sit on it?"

"Are we really stalled, Will?" asked the girl.

"Looks like it--for a while. I'll have to telephone Peters to bring down a tire. Of course, to-day is the day we didn't take it!"

Some minutes later the girl found herself on the cool piazza, in charge of a wonderfully hospitable old lady, while down the road the good-looking young fellow was making long strides toward the next house and a telephone.

"We are staying at the Lindsays', in North Belton," explained the girl, when he was gone, "and we came out for a little spin before dinner. Isn't this Belton? I have an aunt who used to live here somewhere--Aunt Jane Pendergast"

The old lady sat suddenly erect in her chair.

"My dear," she cried, "you don't mean to say that you're Jane Pendergast's niece! Now, that is queer! Why, this was her very house--we bought it when the old gentleman died last year. But, come, we'll go inside. You'll want to see everything, of course!"

It was some time before the young man came back from telephoning, and it was longer still before Peters came with the new tire, and helped get the touring-car ready for the road. The girl was very quiet when they finally left the house, and there was a troubled look deep in her eyes.

"Why, Belle, what's the matter?" asked the young fellow concernedly, as he slackened speed in the cool twilight of the woods, some minutes later. "What's troubling you, dear?"

"Will"--the girl's voice shook--"Will, that was Aunt Jane's house. That old lady--told me."

"Aunt Jane?"

"Yes, yes--the little gray-haired woman that came to live with us two months ago. You know her."

"Why, y-yes; I think I've--seen her."

The girl winced, as from a blow.

"Will, don't! I can't bear it," she choked. "It only shows how we've treated her--how little we've made of her, when we ought to have done everything--everything to make her happy. Instead of that, we were brutes--all of us!"

"Belle!"--the tone was an indignant protest.

"But we were--listen! She lived in that house all her life till last year. She never went anywhere or did anything. For twenty years she lived with an old man who had lost his mind, and she tended him like a baby--only a baby grows older all the time and more interesting, while he--oh, Will, it was awful! That old lady--told me."

"By Jove!" exclaimed the young fellow, under his breath.

"And there were other things," hurried on the girl, tremulously. "Some way, I never thought of Aunt Jane only as old and timid; but she was young like us, once. She wanted to go away to school--but she couldn't go; and there was some one who--loved her--once--later, and she sent him--away. That was after--after grandfather lost his mind. Mother and Uncle Edgar and Uncle Fred--they all went away and lived their own lives, but she stayed on. Then last year grandfather died."

The girl paused and moistened her lips. The man did not speak. His eyes were on the road ahead of the slow-moving car.

"I heard to-day--how--how proud and happy Aunt Jane was that Uncle Fred had asked her to come and live with him," resumed the girl, after a minute. "That old lady told me how Aunt Jane talked and talked about it before she went away, and how she said that all her life she had taken care of others, and it would be so good to feel that now some one was going to look out for her, though, of course, she should do everything she could to help, and she hoped she could still be of some use."

"Well, she has been, hasn't she?"

The girl shook her head.

"That's the worst of it. We haven't made her think she was. She stayed at Uncle Fred's for a while, and then he sent her to Uncle Edgar's. Something must have been wrong there, for she asked mother two months ago if she might come to us."

"Well, I'm sure you've been--good to her."

"But we haven't!" cried the girl. "Mother meant all right, I know, but she didn't think. And I've been--horrid. Aunt Jane tried to show her interest in my wedding plans, but I only laughed at her and said she wouldn't understand. We've pushed her aside, always,--we've never made her one of us; and--we've always made her feel her dependence."

"But you'll do differently now, dear,--now that you understand."

Again the girl shook her head.

"We can't," she moaned. "It's too late. I had a letter from mother last night. Aunt Jane's sick--awfully sick. Mother said I might expect to--to hear of the end any day."

"But there's some time left--a little!"--his voice broke and choked into silence. Suddenly he made a quick movement, and the car beneath them leaped forward like a charger that feels the prick of the spur.

The girl gave a frightened cry, then a tremulous little sob of joy. The man had cried in her ear, in response to her questioning eyes:

"We're--going--to--Aunt Jane!"

And to them both, at the moment, there seemed to be waiting at the end of the road a little bent old woman, into whose wistful eyes they were to bring the light of joy and peace.

ACROSS THE YEARS BY ELEANOR H. PORTER

A Couple of Capitalists

On the top of the hill stood the big brick house--a mansion, compared to the other houses of the New England village. At the foot of the hill nestled the tiny brown farmhouse, half buried in lilacs, climbing roses, and hollyhocks.

Years ago, when Reuben had first brought Emily to that little brown cottage, he had said to her, ruefully: "Sweetheart, 'tain't much of a place, I know, but we'll save and save, every cent we can get, an' by an' by we'll go up to live in the big house on the hill!" And he kissed so tenderly the pretty little woman he had married only that morning that she smiled brightly and declared that the small brown house was the very nicest place in the world.

But, as time passed, the "big house" came to be the Mecca of all their hopes, and penny by penny the savings grew. It was slow work, though, and to hearts less courageous the thing would have seemed an impossibility. No luxuries--and scarcely the bare necessities of life-- came to the little house under the hill, but every month a tiny sum found its way into the savings bank. Fortunately, air and sunshine were cheap, and, if inside the house there was lack of beauty and cheer, outside there was a riotous wealth of color and bloom--the flowers under Emily's loving care flourished and multiplied.

The few gowns in the modest trousseau had been turned inside out and upside down, only to be dyed and turned and twisted all over again. But what was a dyed gown, when one had all that money in the bank and the big house on the hill in prospect! Reuben's best suit grew rusty and seedy, but the man patiently, even gleefully, wore it as long as it would hang together; and when the time came that new garments must be bought for both husband and wife, only the cheapest and flimsiest of material was purchased--but the money in the bank grew.

Reuben never smoked. While other men used the fragrant weed to calm their weary brains and bodies, Reuben--ate peanuts. It had been a curious passion of his, from the time when as a boy he was first presented with a penny for his very own, to spend all his spare cash on this peculiar luxury; and the slow munching of this plebeian delicacy had the same soothing effect on him that a good cigar or an old clay pipe had upon his brother-man. But from the day of his marriage all this was changed; the dimes and the nickels bought no more peanuts, but went to swell the common fund.

It is doubtful if even this heroic economy would have accomplished the desired end had not a certain railroad company cast envious eyes upon the level valley and forthwith sent long arms of steel bearing a puffing engine up through the quiet village. A large tract of waste land belonging to Reuben Gray suddenly became surprisingly valuable, and a sum that trebled twice over the scanty savings of years grew all in a night.

One crisp October day, Mr. and Mrs. Reuben Gray awoke to the fact that they were a little under sixty years of age, and in possession of more than the big sum of money necessary to enable them to carry out the dreams of their youth. They began joyous preparations at once.

The big brick house at the top of the hill had changed hands twice during the last forty years, and the present owner expressed himself as nothing loath to part, not only with the house itself, but with many of its furnishings; and before the winter snow fell the little brown cottage was sold to a thrifty young couple from the neighboring village, and the Grays took up their abode in their new home.

"Well, Em'ly, this is livin', now, ain't it?" said Reuben, as he carefully let himself down into the depths of a velvet-covered chair in the great parlor. "My! ain't this nice!"

"Just perfectly lovely," quavered the thin voice of his wife, as she threw a surreptitious glance at Reuben's shoes to see if they were quite clean enough for such sacred precincts.

It was their first evening in their new abode, and they were a little weary, for they had spent the entire day in exploring every room, peering into every closet, and trying every chair that the establishment contained. It was still quite early when they trudged anxiously about the house, intent on fastening the numerous doors and windows.

"Dear me!" exclaimed the little woman nervously, "I'm 'most afraid to go to bed, Reuben, for fear some one will break in an' steal all these nice things."

"Well, you can sit up if you want to," replied her husband dryly, "but I shall go to bed. Most of these things have been here nigh on to twenty years, an' I guess they'll last the night through." And he marched solemnly upstairs to the big east chamber, meekly followed by his wife.

It was the next morning when Mrs. Gray was washing the breakfast dishes that her husband came in at the kitchen door and stood looking thoughtfully at her.

"Say, Emily," said he, "you'd oughter have a hired girl. 'T ain't your place to be doin' work like this now."

Mrs. Gray gasped--half terrified, half pleased--and shook her head; but her husband was not to be silenced.

"Well, you had--an' you've got to, too. An' you must buy some new clothes--lots of 'em! Why, Em'ly, we've got heaps of money now, an' we hadn't oughter wear such lookin' things."

Emily nodded; she had thought of this before. And the hired-girl hint must have found a warm spot in her heart in which to grow, for that very afternoon she sallied forth, intent on a visit to her counselor on all occasions--the doctor's wife.

"Well, Mis' Steele, I don't know what to do. Reuben says I ought to have a hired girl; but I hain't no more idea where to get one than anything, an' I don't know's I want one, if I did."

And Mrs. Gray sat back in her chair and rocked violently to and fro, eying her hostess with the evident consciousness of having presented a poser. That resourceful woman, however, was far from being nonplussed; she beamed upon her visitor with a joyful smile.

"Just the thing, my dear Mrs. Gray! You know I am to go South with May for the winter. The house will be closed and the doctor at the hotel. I had just been wondering what to do with Nancy, for I want her again in the spring. Now, you can have her until then, and by that time you will know how you like the idea of keeping a girl. She is a perfect treasure, capable of carrying along the entire work of the household, only"--and Mrs. Steele paused long enough to look doubtfully at her friend--"she is a little independent, and won't stand much interference."

Fifteen minutes later Mrs. Gray departed, well pleased though withal a little frightened. She spent the rest of the afternoon in trying to decide between a black alpaca and a green cashmere dress.

That night Reuben brought home a large bag of peanuts and put them down in triumph on the kitchen table.

"There!" he announced in high glee, "I'm goin' to have a bang-up good time!"

"Why, Reuben," remonstrated his wife gently, "you can't eat them things-- you hain't got no teeth to chew 'em with!"

The man's lower jaw dropped.

"Well, I'm a-goin' to try it, anyhow," he insisted. And try he did; but the way his poor old stomach rebelled against the half-masticated things effectually prevented a repetition of the feast.

Early on Monday morning Nancy appeared. Mrs. Gray assumed a brave aspect, but she quaked in her shoes as she showed the big strapping girl to her room. Five minutes later Nancy came into the kitchen to find Mrs. Gray bending over an obstinate coal fire in the range--with neither coal nor range was the little woman in the least familiar.

"There, now," said Nancy briskly, "I'll fix that. You just tell me what you want for dinner, and I can find the things myself." And she attacked the stove with such a clatter and din that Mrs. Gray retreated in terror, murmuring "ham and eggs, if you please," as she fled through the door. Once in the parlor, she seated herself in the middle of the room and thought how nice it was not to get dinner; but she jumped nervously at every sound from the kitchen.

On Tuesday she had mastered her fear sufficiently to go into the kitchen and make a cottage cheese. She did not notice the unfavorable glances of her maid-of-all-work. Wednesday morning she spent happily puttering over "doing up" some handkerchiefs, and she wondered why Nancy kept banging the oven door so often. Thursday she made a special kind of pie that Reuben liked, and remarked pointedly to Nancy that she herself never washed dishes without wearing an extra apron; furthermore, she always placed the pans the other way in the sink. Friday she rearranged the tins on the pantry shelves, that Nancy had so unaccountably mussed up. On Saturday the inevitable explosion came:

"If you please, mum, I'm willin' to do your work, but seems to me it don't make no difference to you whether I wear one apron or six, or whether I hang my dish-towels on a string or on the bars, or whether I wash goblets or kittles first; and I ain't in the habit of havin' folks spyin' round on me. If you want me to go, I'll go; but if I stay, I want to be let alone!"

Poor little Mrs. Gray fled to her seat in the parlor, and for the rest of that winter she did not dare to call her soul her own; but her table was beautifully set and served, and her house was as neat as wax.

The weeks passed and Reuben began to be restless. One day he came in from the post office fairly bubbling over with excitement.

"Say, Em'ly, when folks have money they travel. Let's go somewhere!"

"Why, Reuben--where?" quavered his wife, dropping into the nearest chair.

"Oh, I dunno," with cheerful vagueness; then, suddenly animated, "Let's go to Boston and see the sights!"

"But, Reuben, we don't know no one there," ventured his wife doubtfully.

"Pooh! What if we don't? Hain't we got money? Can't we stay at a hotel? Well, I guess we can!"

And his overwhelming courage put some semblance of confidence into the more timid heart of his wife, until by the end of the week she was as eager as he.

Nancy was tremblingly requested to take a two weeks' vacation, and great was the rejoicing when she graciously acquiesced.

On a bright February morning the journey began. It was not a long one-- four hours only--and the time flew by as on wings of the wind. Reuben assumed an air of worldly wisdom, quite awe-inspiring to his wife. He had visited Boston as a boy, and so had a dim idea of what to expect; moreover, he had sold stock and produce in the large towns near his home, and on the whole felt quite self-sufficient.

As the long train drew into the station, and they alighted and followed the crowd, Mrs. Gray looked with round eyes of wonder at the people--she had not realized that there were so many in the world, and she clung closer and closer to Reuben, who was marching along with a fine show of indifference.

"There," said he, as he deposited his wife and his bags in a seat in the huge waiting-room; "now you stay right here, an' don't you move. I'm goin' to find out about hotels and things."

He was gone so long that she was nearly fainting from fright before she spied his dear form coming toward her. His thin, plain face looked wonderfully beautiful to her, and she almost hugged him right before all those people.

"Well, I've got a hotel all right; but I hain't been here for so long I've kinder forgot about the streets, so the man said we'd better have a team to take us there." And he picked up the bags and trudged off, closely followed by Emily.

His shrewd Yankee wit carried him safely through a bargain with the driver, and they were soon jolting and rumbling along to their destination. He had asked the man behind the news-stand about a hotel, casually mentioning that he had money--plenty of it--and wanted a "bang-up good place." The spirit of mischief had entered the heart of the news-man, and he had given Reuben the name of one of the very highest-priced, most luxurious hotels in the city.

As the carriage stopped, Reuben marched boldly up the broad steps and entered the palatial office, with Emily close at his heels. Two bell-boys sprang forward--the one to take the bags, the other to offer to show Mrs. Gray to the reception-room.

"No, thank you, I ain't particular," said she sweetly; "I'll wait for Reuben here." And she dropped into the nearest chair, while her husband advanced toward the desk. She noticed that men were looking curiously at her, and she felt relieved when Reuben and the pretty boy came back and said they would go up to their room.

She stood the elevator pretty well, though she gave a little gasp (which she tried to choke into a cough) as it started. Reuben turned to the boy.

"Where can I get somethin' to eat?"

"Luncheon is being served in the main dining-room on the first floor, sir."

Visions of a lunch as he knew it in Emily's pantry came to him, and he looked a little dubious.

"Well, I'm pretty hungry; but if that's all I can get I suppose it will have to do."

Ten minutes later an officious head waiter, whom Emily looked upon with timid awe, was seating them in a superbly appointed dining-room. Reuben looked at the menu doubtfully, while an attentive, soft-voiced man at his elbow bent low to catch his order. Few of the strange-looking words conveyed any sort of meaning to the poor hungry man. At length spying "chicken" halfway down the card, he pointed to it in relief.

"I guess I'll take some of that," he said, briefly; then he added, "I don't know how much it costs--you hain't got no price after it."

The waiter comprehended at once.

"The luncheon is served in courses, sir; you pay for the whole--whether you eat it or not," he added shrewdly. "If you will let me serve you according to my judgment, sir, I think I can please you."

And there the forlorn little couple sat, amazed and hungry, through six courses, each one of which seemed to their uneducated palate one degree worse than the last.

Two hours later they started for a long walk down the wonderful, fascinating street. Each marvelous window display came in for its full share of attention, but they stood longest before bakeries and restaurants. Finally, upon coming to one of the latter, where an enticing sign announced "Boiled Dinner To-day, Served Hot at All Hours," Reuben could endure it no longer.

"By Jinks, Em'ly, I've just got to have some of that. That stodged-up mess I ate at the hotel didn't go to the spot at all. Come on, let's have a good square meal."

The hotel knew them just one night. The next morning before breakfast Reuben manfully paid his--to him astounding--bill and departed for more congenial quarters, which they soon found on a neighboring side street.

The rest of the visit was, of course, delightful, only the streets were pretty crowded and noisy, and they couldn't sleep very well at night; moreover, Reuben lost his pocketbook with a small sum of money in it; so, on the whole, they concluded to go home a little before the two weeks ended.

When spring came Nancy returned to her former mistress, and her vacant throne remained unoccupied. Little by little the dust gathered on the big velvet chairs in the parlor, and the room was opened less and less. When the first green things commenced to send tender shoots up through the wet, brown earth, Reuben's restlessness was very noticeable. By and by he began to go off very early in the morning, returning at noon for a hasty dinner, then away again till night. To his wife's repeated questioning he would reply, sheepishly, "Oh, just loafin', that's all."

And Emily was nervous, too. Of late she had taken a great fancy to a daily walk, and it always led in one direction--down past the little brown house. Of course, she glanced over the fence at the roses and lilacs, and she couldn't help seeing that they all looked sadly neglected. By and by the weeds came, grew, and multiplied; and every time she passed the gate her throat fairly choked in sympathy with her old pets.

Evenings, she and Reuben spent very happily on the back stoop, talking of their great good fortune in being able to live in such a fine large house. Somehow they said more than usual about it this spring, and Reuben often mentioned how glad he was that his wife didn't have to dig in the garden any more; and Emily would reply that she, too, was glad that he was having so easy a time. Then they would look down at the little brown farmhouse and wonder how they ever managed to get along in so tiny a place.

One day, in passing this same little house, Emily stopped a moment and leaned over the gate, that she might gain a better view of her favorite rosebush.

She evinced the same interest the next two mornings, and on the third she timidly opened the gate and walked up the old path to the door. A buxom woman with a big baby in her arms, and a bigger one hanging to her skirts, answered her knock.

"How do you do, Mis' Gray. Won't you come in?" said she civilly, looking mildly surprised.

"No, thank you--yes--I mean--I came to see you," stammered Emily confusedly.

"You're very good," murmured the woman, still standing in the doorway.

"Your flowers are so pretty," ventured Mrs. Gray, unable to keep the wistfulness out of her voice.

"Do you think so?" carelessly; "I s'pose they need weedin'. What with my babies an' all, I don't get much time for posies."

"Oh, please,--would it be too much trouble to let me come an' putter around in the beds?" queried the little woman eagerly. "Oh, I would like it so much!"

The other laughed heartily.

"Well, I really don't see how it's goin' to trouble me to have you weedin' my flowers; in fact, I should think the shoe would be on the other foot." Then the red showed in her face a little. "You're welcome to do whatever you want, Mis' Gray."

"Oh, thank you!" exclaimed Emily, as she quickly pulled up an enormous weed at her feet.

It took but a few hours' work to bring about a wonderfully happy change in that forlorn garden, and then Mrs. Gray found that she had a big pile of weeds to dispose of. Filling her apron with a portion of them, she started to go behind the house in search of a garbage heap. Around the corner she came face to face with her husband, hoe in hand.

"Why, Reuben Gray! Whatever in the world are you doing?"

For a moment the man was crushed with the enormity of his crime; then he caught sight of his wife's dirt-stained fingers.

"Well, I guess I ain't doin' no worse than you be!" And he turned his back and began to hoe vigorously.

Emily dropped the weeds where she stood, turned about, and walked through the garden and up the hill, pondering many things.

Supper was strangely quiet that night. Mrs. Gray had asked a single question: "Reuben, do you want the little house back?"

A glad light leaped into the old man's eyes.

"Em'ly--would you be willin' to?"

After the supper dishes were put away, Mrs. Gray, with a light shawl over her head, came to her husband on the back stoop.

"Come, dear; I think we'd better go down to-night."

A few minutes later they sat stiffly in the best room of the farmhouse, while the buxom woman and her husband looked wonderingly at them.

"You wan't thinkin' of sellin', was ye?" began Reuben insinuatingly.

The younger man's eyelid quivered a little. "Well, no,--I can't hardly say that I was. I hain't but just bought."

Reuben hitched his chair a bit and glanced at Emily.

"Well, me and my wife have concluded that we're too old to transplant-- we don't seem to take root very easy--and we've been thinkin'--would you swap even, now?"

It must have been a month later that Reuben Gray and his wife were contentedly sitting in the old familiar kitchen of the little brown house.

"I've been wondering, Reuben," said his wife--"I've been wondering if 'twouldn't have been just as well if we'd taken some of the good things while they was goin'--before we got too old to enjoy 'em."

"Yes--peanuts, for instance," acquiesced her husband ruefully.

ACROSS THE YEARS BY ELEANOR H. PORTER

In the Footsteps of Katy

Only Alma had lived--Alma, the last born. The other five, one after another, had slipped from loving, clinging arms into the great Silence, leaving worse than a silence behind them; and neither Nathan Kelsey nor his wife Mary could have told you which hurt the more,--the saying of a last good-bye to a stalwart, grown lad of twenty, or the folding of tiny, waxen hands over a heart that had not counted a year of beating. Yet both had fallen to their lot.

As for Alma--Alma carried in her dainty self all the love, hopes, tenderness, ambitions, and prayers that otherwise would have been bestowed upon six. And Alma was coming home.

"Mary," said Nathan one June evening, as he and his wife sat on the back porch, "I saw Jim Hopkins ter-day. Katy's got home."

"Hm-m,"--the low rocker swayed gently to and fro,--"Katy's been ter college, same as Alma, ye know."

"Yes; an'--an' that's what Jim was talkin' 'bout He was feelin' bad-powerful bad."

"Bad!"--the rocker stopped abruptly. "Why, Nathan!"

"Yes; he--" There was a pause, then the words came with the rush of desperation. "He said home wan't like home no more. That Katy was as good as gold, an' they was proud of her; but she was turrible upsettin'. Jim has ter rig up nights now ter eat supper--put on his coat an' a b'iled collar; an' he says he's got so he don't dast ter open his head. They're all so, too--Mis' Hopkins, an' Sue, an' Aunt Jane--don't none of 'em dast ter speak."

"Why, Nathan!--why not?"

"'Cause of--Katy. Jim says there don't nothin' they say suit Katy--'bout its wordin', I mean. She changes it an' tells 'em what they'd orter said."

"Why, the saucy little baggage!"--the rocker resumed its swaying, and Mary Kelsey's foot came down on the porch floor with decided, rhythmic pats.

The man stirred restlessly.

"But she ain't sassy, Mary," he demurred. "Jim says Katy's that sweet an' pleasant about it that ye can't do nothin'. She tells 'em she's kerrectin' 'em fur their own good, an' that they need culturin'. An' Jim says she spends all o' meal-time tellin' 'bout the things on the table,--salt, an' where folks git it, an' pepper, an' tumblers, an' how folks make 'em. He says at first 'twas kind o' nice an' he liked ter hear it; but now, seems as if he hain't got no appetite left ev'ry time he sets down ter the table. He don't relish eatin' such big words an' queer names."

"An' that ain't all," resumed Nathan, after a pause for breath. "Jim can't go hoein' nor diggin' but she'll foller him an' tell 'bout the bugs an' worms he turns up,--how many legs they've got, an' all that. An' the moon ain't jest a moon no more, an' the stars ain't stars. They're sp'eres an' planets with heathenish names an' rings an' orbits. Jim feels bad--powerful bad--'bout it, an' he says he can't see no way out of it. He knows they hain't had much schooling any of 'em, only Katy, an' he says that sometimes he 'most wishes that--that she hadn't, neither."

Nathan Kelsey's voice had sunk almost to a whisper, and with the last words his eyes sent a furtive glance toward the stoop-shouldered little figure in the low rocker. The chair was motionless now, and its occupant sat picking at a loose thread in the gingham apron.

"I--I wouldn't 'a' spoke of it," stammered the man, with painful hesitation, "only--well, ye see, I--you-" he stopped helplessly.

"I know," faltered the little woman. "You was thinkin' of--Alma."

"She wouldn't do it--Alma wouldn't!" retorted the man sharply, almost before his wife had ceased speaking.

"No, no, of course not; but--Nathan, ye don't think Alma'd ever be--ashamed of us, do ye?"

"'Course not!" asserted Nathan, but his voice shook. "Don't ye worry, Mary," he comforted. "Alma ain't a-goin' ter do no kerrectin' of us."

"Nathan, I--I think that's 'co-rectin',"' suggested the woman, a little breathlessly.

The man turned and gazed at his wife without speaking. Then his jaw fell.

"Well, by sugar, Mary! You ain't a-goin' ter begin it, be ye?" he demanded.

"Why, no, 'course not!" she laughed confusedly. "An'--an' Alma wouldn't."

"'Course Alma wouldn't," echoed her husband. "Come, it's time ter shut up the house."

The date of Alma's expected arrival was yet a week ahead.

As the days passed, there came a curious restlessness to the movements of both Nathan and his wife. It was on the last night of that week of waiting that Mrs. Kelsey spoke.

"Nathan," she began, with forced courage, "I've been over to Mis' Hopkins's--an' asked her what special things 'twas that Katy set such store by. I thought mebbe if we knew 'em beforehand, an' could do 'em, an'--"

"That's jest what I asked Jim ter-day, Mary," cut in Nathan excitedly.

"Nathan, you didn't, now! Oh, I'm so glad! An' we'll do 'em, won't we?-- jest ter please her?"

"'Course we will!"

"Ye see it's four years since she was here, Nathan, what with her teachin' summers."

"Sugar, now! Is it? It hain't seemed so long."

"Nathan," interposed Mrs. Kelsey, anxiously, "I think that 'hain't' ain't--I mean aren't right. I think you'd orter say, 'It haven't seemed so long.'"

The man frowned, and made an impatient gesture.

"Yes, yes, I know," soothed his wife; "but,--well, we might jest as well begin now an' git used to it. Mis' Hopkins said that them two words, 'hain't an' 'ain't, was what Katy hated most of anythin'."

"Yes; Jim mentioned 'em, too," acknowledged Nathan gloomily. "But he said that even them wan't half so bad as his riggin' up nights. He said that Katy said that after the 'toil of the day' they must 'don fresh garments an' come ter the evenin' meal with minds an' bodies refreshed.'"

"Yes; an', Nathan, ain't my black silk--"

"Ahem! I'm a-thinkin' it wa'n't me that said 'ain't' that time," interposed Nathan.

"Dear, dear, Nathan!--did I? Oh, dear, what will Alma say?"

"It don't make no diff'rence what Alma says, Mary. Don't ye fret," returned the man with sudden sharpness, as he rose to his feet. "I guess Alma'll have ter take us 'bout as we be-- 'bout as we be."

Yet it was Nathan who asked, just as his wife was dropping off to sleep that night:--

"Mary, is it three o' them collars I've got, or four?--b'iled ones, I mean."

At five o'clock the next afternoon Mrs. Kelsey put on the treasured black silk dress, sacred for a dozen years to church, weddings, and funerals. Nathan, warm and uncomfortable in his Sunday suit and stiff collar, had long since driven to the station for Alma. The house, brushed and scrubbed into a state of speckless order, was thrown wide open to welcome the returning daughter. At a quarter before six she came.

"Mother, you darling!" cried a voice, and Mrs. Kelsey found herself in the clasp of strong young arms, and gazing into a flushed, eager face. "Don't you look good! And doesn't everything look good!" finished the girl.

"Does it--I mean, do it?" quavered the little woman excitedly. "Oh, Alma, I am glad ter see ye!"

Behind Alma's back Nathan flicked a bit of dust from his coat. The next instant he raised a furtive hand and gave his collar and neckband a savage pull.

At the supper-table that night ten minutes of eager questioning on the part of Alma had gone by before Mrs. Kelsey realized that thus far their conversation had been of nothing more important than Nathan's rheumatism, her own health, and the welfare of Rover, Tabby, and the mare Topsy. Commensurate with the happiness that had been hers during those ten minutes came now her remorse. She hastened to make amends.

"There, there, Alma, I beg yer pardon, I'm sure. I hain't--er--I haven't meant ter keep ye talkin' on such triflin' things, dear. Now talk ter us yer self. Tell us about things-- anythin'--anythin' on the table or in the room," she finished feverishly.

For a moment the merry-faced girl stared in frank amazement at her mother; then she laughed gleefully.

"On the table? In the room?" she retorted. "Well, it's the dearest room ever, and looks so good to me! As for the table--the rolls are feathers, the coffee is nectar, and the strawberries--well, the strawberries are just strawberries--they couldn't be nicer."

"Oh, Alma, but I didn't mean----"

"Tut, tut, tut!" interrupted Alma laughingly. "Just as if the cook didn't like her handiwork praised! Why, when I draw a picture--oh, and I haven't told you!" she broke off excitedly. The next instant she was on her feet. "Alma Mead Kelsey, Illustrator; at your service," she announced with a low bow. Then she dropped into her seat again and went on speaking.

"You see, I've been doing this sort of thing for some time," she explained, "and have had some success in selling. My teacher has always encouraged me, and, acting on his advice, I stayed over in New York a week with a friend, and took some of my work to the big publishing houses. That's why I didn't get here as soon as Kate Hopkins did. I hated to put off my coming; but now I'm so glad I did. Only think! I sold every single thing, and I have orders and orders ahead."

"Well, by sugar!" ejaculated the man at the head of the table.

"Oh-h-h!" breathed the little woman opposite. "Oh, Alma, I'm so glad!"

In spite of Mrs. Kelsey's protests that night after supper, Alma tripped about the kitchen and pantry wiping the dishes and putting them away. At dusk father, mother, and daughter seated themselves on the back porch.

"There!" sighed Alma. "Isn't this restful? And isn't that moon glorious?"

Mrs. Kelsey shot a quick look at her husband; then she cleared her throat nervously.

"Er--yes," she assented. "I--I s'pose you know what it's made of, an' how big 'tis, an'--an' what there is on it, don't ye, Alma?"

Alma raised her eyebrows.

"Hm-m; well, there are still a few points that I and the astronomers haven't quite settled," she returned, with a whimsical smile.

"An' the stars, they've got names, I s'pose--every one of 'em," proceeded Mrs. Kelsey, so intent on her own part that Alma's reply passed unnoticed.

Alma laughed; then she assumed an attitude of mock rapture, and quoted:

  "'Scintillate, scintillate, globule vivific,
   Fain would I fathom thy nature specific;
   Loftily poised in ether capacious,
   Strongly resembling the gem carbonaceous.'"

There was a long silence. Alma's eyes were on the flying clouds.

"Would--would you mind saying that again, Alma?" asked Mrs. Kelsey at last timidly.

Alma turned with a start.

"Saying what, dearie?--oh, that nonsensical verse? Of course not! That's only another way of saying 'twinkle, twinkle, little star.' Means just the same, only uses up a few more letters to make the words. Listen." And she repeated the two, line for line.

"Oh!" said her mother faintly. "Er--thank you."

"I--I guess I'll go to bed," announced Nathan Kelsey suddenly.

The next morning Alma's pleadings were in vain. Mrs. Kelsey insisted that Alma should go about her sketching, leaving the housework for her own hands to perform. With a laughing protest and a playful pout, Alma tucked her sketchbook under her arm and left the house to go down by the river. In the field she came upon her father.

"Hard at work, dad?" she called affectionately. "Old Mother Earth won't yield her increase without just so much labor, will she?"

"That she won't," laughed the man. Then he flushed a quick red and set a light foot on a crawling thing of many legs which had emerged from beneath an overturned stone.

"Oh!" cried Alma. "Your foot, father--your're crushing something!"

The flush grew deeper.

"Oh, I guess not," rejoined the man, lifting his foot, and giving a curiously resigned sigh as he sent an apprehensive glance into the girl's face.

"Dear, dear! isn't he funny?" murmured the girl, bending low and giving a gentle poke with the pencil in her hand. "Only fancy," she added, straightening herself, "only fancy if we had so many feet. Just picture the size of our shoe bill!" And she laughed and turned away.

"Well, by gum!" ejaculated the man, looking after her. Then he fell to work, and his whistle, as he worked, carried something of the song of a bird set free from a cage.

A week passed.

The days were spent by Alma in roaming the woods and fields, pencil and paper in hand; they were spent by her mother in the hot kitchen over a hotter stove. To Alma's protests and pleadings Mrs. Kelsey was deaf. Alma's place was not there, her work was not housework, declared Alma's mother.

On Mrs. Kelsey the strain was beginning to tell. It was not the work alone--though that was no light matter, owing to her anxiety that Alma's pleasure and comfort should find nothing wanting--it was more than the work.

Every night at six the anxious little woman, flushed from biscuit-baking and chicken-broiling and almost sick with fatigue, got out the black silk gown and the white lace collar and put them on with trembling hands. Thus robed in state she descended to the supper-table, there to confront her husband still more miserable in the stiff collar and black coat.

Nor yet was this all. Neither the work nor the black silk dress contained for Mrs. Kelsey quite the possibilities of soul torture that were to be found in the words that fell from her lips. As the days passed, the task the little woman had set for herself became more and more hopeless, until she scarcely could bring herself to speak at all, so stumbling and halting were her sentences.

At the end of the eighth day came the culmination of it all. Alma, her nose sniffing the air, ran into the kitchen that night to find no one in the room, and the biscuits burning in the oven. She removed the biscuits, threw wide the doors and windows, then hurried upstairs to her mother's room.

"Why, mother!"

Mrs. Kelsey stood before the glass, a deep flush on her cheeks and tears rolling down her face. Two trembling hands struggled with the lace at her throat until the sharp point of a pin found her thumb and left a tiny crimson stain on the spotlessness of the collar. It was then that Mrs. Kelsey covered her face with her hands and sank into the low chair by the bed.

"Why, mother!" cried Alma again, hurrying across the room and dropping on her knees at her mother's side.

"I can't, Alma, I can't!" moaned the woman. "I've tried an' tried; but I've got ter give up, I've got ter give up."

"Can't what, dearie?--give up what?" demanded Alma.

Mrs. Kelsey shook her head. Then she dropped her hands and looked fearfully into her daughter's face.

"An' yer father, too, Alma--he's tried, an' he can't," she choked.

"Tried what? What do you mean?"

With her eyes on Alma's troubled, amazed face, Mrs. Kelsey made one last effort to gain her lost position. She raised her shaking hands to her throat and fumbled for the pin and the collar.

"There, there, dear, don't fret," she stammered. "I didn't think what I was sayin'. It ain't nothin'--I mean, it aren't nothin'--it am not--oh-h!" she sobbed; "there, ye see, Alma, I can't, I can't. It ain't no more use ter try!" Down went the gray head on Alma's strong young shoulder.

"There, there, dear, cry away," comforted Alma, with loving pats. "It will do you good; then we'll hear what this is all about, from the very beginning."

And Mrs. Kelsey told her--and from the very beginning. When the telling was over, and the little woman, a bit breathless and frightened, sat awaiting what Alma would say, there came a long silence.

Alma's lips were close shut. Alma was not quite sure, if she opened them, whether there would come a laugh or a sob. The laugh was uppermost and almost parted the firm-set lips, when a side glance at the quivering face of the little woman in the big chair turned the laugh into a half-stifled sob. Then Alma spoke.

"Mother, dear, listen. Do you think a silk dress and a stiff collar can make you and father any dearer to me? Do you think an 'ain't' or a 'hain't' can make me love either of you any less? Do you suppose I expect you, after fifty years' service for others, to be as careful in your ways and words as if you'd spent those fifty years in training yourself instead of in training six children? Why, mother, dear, do you suppose that I don't know that for twenty of those years you have had no thoughts, no prayers, save for me?--that I have been the very apple of your eye? Well, it's my turn, now, and you are the apple of my eye--you and father. Why, dearie, you have no idea of the plans I have for you. There's a good strong woman coming next week for the kitchen work. Oh, it's all right," assured Alma, quickly, in response to the look on her mother's face. "Why, I'm rich! Only think of those orders! And then you shall dress in silk or velvet, or calico--anything you like, so long as it doesn't scratch nor prick," she added merrily, bending forward and fastening the lace collar. "And you shall----"

"Ma-ry?" It was Nathan at the foot of the back stairway.

"Yes, Nathan."

"Ain't it 'most supper-time?"

"Bless my soul!" cried Mrs. Kelsey, springing to her feet.

"An', Mary----"

"Yes."

"Hain't I got a collar--a b'iled one, on the bureau up there?"

"No," called Alma, snatching up the collar and throwing it on the bed. "There isn't a sign of one there. Suppose you let it go to-night, dad?"

"Well, if you don't mind!" And a very audible sigh of relief floated up the back stairway.

The Bridge Across the Years

John was expected on the five o'clock stage. Mrs. John had been there three days now, and John's father and mother were almost packed up--so Mrs. John said. The auction would be to-morrow at nine o'clock, and with John there to see that things "hustled"-- which last was really unnecessary to mention, for John's very presence meant "hustle"--

with John there, then, the whole thing ought to be over by one o'clock, and they off in season to 'catch the afternoon express.

And what a time it had been--those three days!

Mrs. John, resting in the big chair on the front porch, thought of those days with complacency--that they were over. Grandpa and Grandma Burton, hovering over old treasures in the attic, thought of them with terrified dismay--that they had ever begun.

I am coming up on Tuesday [Mrs. John had written]. We have been thinking for some time that you and father ought not to be left alone up there on the farm any longer. Now don't worry about the packing. I shall bring Marie, and you won't have to lift your finger. John will come Thursday night, and be there for the auction on Friday. By that time we shall have picked out what is worth saving, and everything will be ready for him to take matters in hand. I think he has already written to the auctioneer, so tell father to give himself no uneasiness on that score.

John says he thinks we can have you back here with us by Friday night, or Saturday at the latest. You know John's way, so you may be sure there will be no tiresome delay. Your rooms here will be all ready before I leave, so that part will be all right.

This may seem a bit sudden to you, but you know we have always told you that the time was surely coming when you couldn't live alone any longer. John thinks it has come now; and, as I said before, you know John, so, after all, you won't be surprised at his going right ahead with things. We shall do everything possible to make you comfortable, and I am sure you will be very happy here.

Good-bye, then, until Tuesday. With love to both of you.

Edith.

That had been the beginning. To Grandpa and Grandma Burton it had come like a thunderclap on a clear day. They had known, to be sure, that son John frowned a little at their lonely life; but that there should come this sudden transplanting, this ruthless twisting and tearing up of roots that for sixty years had been burrowing deeper and deeper--it was almost beyond one's comprehension.

And there was the auction!

"We shan't need that, anyway," Grandma Burton had said at once. "What few things we don't want to keep I shall give away. An auction, indeed! Pray, what have we to sell?"

"Hm-m! To be sure, to be sure," her husband had murmured; but his face was troubled, and later he had said, apologetically: "You see, Hannah, there's the farm things. We don't need them."

On Tuesday night Mrs. John and the somewhat awesome Maria--to whom Grandpa and Grandma Burton never could learn not to curtsy--arrived; and almost at once Grandma Burton discovered that not only "farm things," but such precious treasures as the hair wreath and the parlor--set were auctionable. In fact, everything the house contained, except their clothing and a few crayon portraits, seemed to be in the same category.

"But, mother, dear," Mrs. John had returned, with a laugh, in response to Grandma Burton's horrified remonstrances, "just wait until you see your rooms, and how full they are of beautiful things, and then you'll understand."

"But they won't be--these," the old voice had quavered.

And Mrs. John had laughed again, and had patted her mother-in-law's cheek, and had echoed-but with a different shade of meaning--"No, they certainly won't be these!"

In the attic now, on a worn black trunk, sat the little old man, and down on the floor before an antiquated cradle knelt his wife.

"They was all rocked in it, Seth," she was saying,--"John and the twins and my two little girls; and now there ain't any one left only John--and the cradle."

"I know, Hannah, but you ain't usin' that nowadays, so you don't really need it," comforted the old man. "But there's my big chair now-- seems as though we jest oughter take that. Why, there ain't a day goes by that I don't set in it!"

"But John's wife says there's better ones there, Seth," soothed the old woman in her turn, "as much as four or five of 'em right in our rooms."

"So she did, so she did!" murmured the man. "I'm an ongrateful thing; so I be." There was a long pause. The old man drummed with his fingers on the trunk and watched a cloud sail across the skylight. The woman gently swung the cradle to and fro. "If only they wan't goin' ter be--sold!" she choked, after a time. "I like ter know that they're where I can look at 'em, an' feel of 'em, an'--an' remember things. Now there's them quilts with all my dress pieces in 'em--a piece of most every dress I've had since I was a girl; an' there's that hair wreath--seems as if I jest couldn't let that go, Seth. Why, there's your hair, an' John's, an' some of the twins', an'--"

"There, there, dear; now I jest wouldn't fret," cut in the old man quickly. "Like enough when you get used ter them other things on the wall you'll like 'em even better than the hair wreath. John's wife says she's taken lots of pains an' fixed 'em up with pictures an' curtains an' everythin' nice," went on Seth, talking very fast. "Why, Hannah, it's you that's bein' ongrateful now, dear!"

"So 'tis, so 'tis, Seth, an' it ain't right an' I know it. I ain't a-goin' ter do so no more; now see!" And she bravely turned her back on the cradle and walked, head erect, toward the attic stairs.

John came at five o'clock. He engulfed the little old man and the little old woman in a bearlike hug, and breezily demanded what they had been doing to themselves to make them look so forlorn. In the very next breath, however, he answered his own question, and declared it was because they had been living all cooped up alone so long--so it was; and that it was high time it was stopped, and that he had come to do it! Whereupon the old man and the old woman smiled bravely and told each other what a good, good son they had, to be sure!

Friday dawned clear, and not too warm--an ideal auction-day. Long before nine o'clock the yard was full of teams and the house of people. Among them all, however, there was no sign of the bent old man and the erect little old woman, the owners of the property to be sold. John and Mrs. John were not a little disturbed--they had lost their father and mother.

Nine o'clock came, and with it began the strident call of the auctioneer. Men laughed and joked over their bids, and women looked on and gossiped, adding a bid of their own now and then. Everywhere was the son of the house, and things went through with a rush. Upstairs, in the darkest corner of the attic--which had been cleared of goods--sat, hand in hand on an old packing-box, a little old man and a little old woman who winced and shrank together every time the "Going, going, gone!" floated up to them from the yard below.

At half-past one the last wagon rumbled out of the yard, and five minutes later Mrs. John gave a relieved cry.

"Oh, there you are! Why, mother, father, where have you been?"

There was no reply. The old man choked back a cough and bent to flick a bit of dust from his coat. The old woman turned and crept away, her erect little figure looking suddenly bent and old.

"Why, what--" began John, as his father, too, turned away. "Why, Edith, you don't suppose--" He stopped with a helpless frown.

"Perfectly natural, my dear, perfectly natural," returned Mrs. John lightly. "We'll get them away immediately. It'll be all right when once they are started."

Some hours later a very tired old man and a still more tired old woman crept into a pair of sumptuous, canopy-topped twin beds. There was only one remark.

"Why, Seth, mine ain't feathers a mite! Is yours?"

There was no reply. Tired nature had triumphed--Seth was asleep.

They made a brave fight, those two. They told themselves that the chairs were easier, the carpets softer, and the pictures prettier than those that had gone under the hammer that day as they sat hand in hand in the attic. They assured each other that the unaccustomed richness of window and bed hangings and the profusion of strange vases and statuettes did not make them afraid to stir lest they soil or break something. They insisted to each other that they were not homesick, and that they were perfectly satisfied as they were. And yet--

When no one was looking Grandpa Burton tried chair after chair, and wondered why there was only one particular chair in the whole world that just exactly "fitted;" and when the twilight hour came Grandma Burton wondered what she would give to be able just to sit by the old cradle and talk with the past.

The newspapers said it was a most marvelous escape for the whole family. They gave a detailed account of how the beautiful residence of the Honorable John Burton, with all its costly furnishings, had burned to the ground, and of how the entire family was saved, making special mention of the honorable gentleman's aged father and mother. No one was injured, fortunately, and the family had taken up a temporary residence in the nearest hotel. It was understood that Mr. Burton would begin rebuilding at once.

The newspapers were right--Mr. Burton did begin rebuilding at once; in fact, the ashes of the Burton mansion were not cold before John Burton began to interview architects and contractors.

"It'll be 'way ahead of the old one," he confided to his wife enthusiastically.

Mrs. John sighed.

"I know, dear," she began plaintively; "but, don't you see? it won't be the same--it can't be. Why, some of those things we've had ever since we were married. They seemed a part of me, John. I was used to them. I had grown up with some of them--those candlesticks of mamma's, for instance, that she had when I was a bit of a baby. Do you think money can buy another pair that--that were hers?" And Mrs. John burst into tears.

"Come, come, dear," protested her husband, with a hasty caress and a nervous glance at the clock--he was due at the bank in ten minutes. "Don't fret about what can't be helped; besides"-and he laughed whimsically--"you must look out or you'll be getting as bad as mother over her hair wreath!" And with another hasty pat on her shoulder he was gone.

Mrs. John suddenly stopped her crying. She lowered her handkerchief and stared fixedly at an old print on the wall opposite. The hotel--though strictly modern in cuisine and management--was an old one, and prided itself on the quaintness of its old-time furnishings. Just what the print represented Mrs. John could not have told, though her eyes did not swerve from its face for five long minutes. What she did see was a silent, dismantled farmhouse, and a little old man and a little old woman with drawn faces and dumb lips.

Was it possible? Had she, indeed, been so blind?

Mrs. John rose to her feet, bathed her eyes, straightened her neck-bow, and crossed the hall to Grandma Burton's room.

"Well, mother, and how are you getting along?" she asked cheerily.

"Jest as nice as can be, daughter,--and ain't this room pretty?" returned the little old woman eagerly. "Do you know, it seems kind of natural like; mebbe it's because of that chair there. Seth says it's almost like his at home."

It was a good beginning, and Mrs. John made the most of it. Under her skillful guidance Grandma Burton, in less than five minutes, had gone from the chair to the old clock which her father used to wind, and from the clock to the bureau where she kept the dead twins' little white shoes and bonnets. She told, too, of the cherished parlor chairs and marble-topped table, and of how she and father had saved and saved for years to buy them; and even now, as she talked, her voice rang with pride of possession--though only for a moment; it shook then with the remembrance of loss.

There was no complaint, it is true, no audible longing for lost treasures. There was only the unwonted joy of pouring into sympathetic ears the story of things loved and lost--things the very mention of which brought sweet faint echoes of voices long since silent.

"There, there," broke off the little old woman at last, "how I am runnin' on! But, somehow, somethin' set me to talkin' ter-day. Mebbe't was that chair that's like yer father's," she hazarded.

"Maybe it was," agreed Mrs. John quietly, as she rose to her feet.

The new house came on apace. In a wonderfully short time John Burton began to urge his wife to see about rugs and hangings. It was then that Mrs. John called him to one side and said a few hurried but very earnest words--words that made the Honorable John open wide his eyes.

"But, Edith," he remonstrated, "are you crazy? It simply couldn't be done! The things are scattered over half a dozen townships; besides, I haven't the least idea where the auctioneer's list is--if I saved it at all."

"Never mind, dear; I may try, surely," begged Mrs. John. And her husband laughed and reached for his check-book.

"Try? Of course you may try! And here's this by way of wishing you good luck," he finished, as he handed her an oblong bit of paper that would go far toward smoothing the most difficult of ways.

"You dear!" cried Mrs. John. "And now I'm going to work."

It was at about this time that Mrs. John went away. The children were at college and boarding-school; John was absorbed in business and house-building, and Grandpa and Grandma Burton were contented and well cared for. There really seemed to be no reason why Mrs. John should not go away, if she wished--and she apparently did wish. It was at about this time, too, that certain Vermont villages--one of which was the Honorable John Burton's birthplace--were stirred to sudden interest and action. A persistent, smiling-faced woman had dropped into their midst--a woman who drove from house to house, and who, in every case, left behind her a sworn ally and friend, pledged to serve her cause.

Little by little, in an unused room in the village hotel there began to accumulate a motley collection--a clock, a marble-topped table, a cradle, a patchwork quilt, a bureau, a hair wreath, a chair worn with age and use. And as this collection grew in size and fame, only that family which could not add to it counted itself abused and unfortunate, so great was the spell that the persistent, smiling-faced woman had cast about her.

Just before the Burton house was finished Mrs. John came back to town. She had to hurry a little about the last of the decorations and furnishings to make up for lost time; but there came a day when the place was pronounced ready for occupancy.

It was then that Mrs. John hurried into Grandpa and Grandma Burton's rooms at the hotel.

"Come, dears," she said gayly. "The house is all ready, and we're going home."

"Done? So soon?" faltered Grandma Burton, who had not been told very much concerning the new home's progress. "Why, how quick they have built it!"

There was a note of regret in the tremulous old voice, but Mrs. John did not seem to notice. The old man, too, rose from his chair with a long sigh--and again Mrs. John did not seem to notice.

"Yes, dearie, yes, it's all very nice and fine," said Grandma Burton wearily, half an hour later as she trudged through the sumptuous parlors and halls of the new house; "but, if you don't mind, I guess I'll go to my room, daughter. I'm tired--turrible tired."

Up the stairs and along the hall trailed the little procession--Mrs. John, John, the bent old man, and the little old woman. At the end of the hall Mrs. John paused a moment, then flung the door wide open.

There was a gasp and a quick step forward; then came the sudden illumination of two wrinkled old faces.

"John! Edith!"--it was a cry of mingled joy and wonder.

There was no reply. Mrs. John had closed the door and left them there with their treasures.

For Jimmy

Uncle Zeke's pipe had gone out--sure sign that Uncle Zeke's mind was not at rest. For five minutes the old man had occupied in frowning silence the other of my veranda rocking-chairs. As I expected, however, I had not long to wait.

"I met old Sam Hadley an' his wife in the cemetery just now," he observed.

"Yes?" I was careful to express just enough, and not too much, interest: one had to be circumspect with Uncle Zeke.

"Hm-m; I was thinkin'--" Uncle Zeke paused, shifted his position, and began again. This time I had the whole story.

"I was thinkin'--I don't say that Jimmy did right, an' I don't say that Jimmy did wrong. Maybe you can tell. 'Twas like this:

"In a way we all claimed Jimmy Hadley. As a little fellow, he was one of them big-eyed, curly-haired chaps that gets inside your heart no matter how tough't is. An' we was really fond of him, too,--so fond of him that we didn't do nothin' but jine in when his pa an' ma talked as if he was the only boy that ever was born, or ever would be--an' you know we must have been purty daft ter stood that, us bein' fathers ourselves!

"Well, as was natural, perhaps, the Hadleys jest lived fer Jimmy. They'd lost three, an' he was all there was left. They wasn't very well-to-do, but nothin' was too grand fer Jimmy, and when the boy begun ter draw them little pictures of his all over the shed an' the barn door, they was plumb crazy. There wan't no doubt of it--Jimmy was goin' ter be famous, they said. He was goin' ter be one o' them painter fellows, an' make big money.

"An' Jimmy did work, even then. He stood well in his studies, an' worked outside, earnin' money so's he could take drawin' lessons when he got bigger. An' by and by he did get bigger, an' he did take lessons down ter the Junction twice a week.

"There wan't no livin' with Mis' Hadley then, she was that proud; an' when he brought home his first picture, they say she never went ter bed at all that night, but jest set gloatin' over it till the sun came in an' made her kerosene lamp look as silly as she did when she saw 'twas mornin'. There was one thing that plagued her, though: 'twan't painted-- that picture. Jimmy called it a 'black an' white,' an' said 'twan't paintin' that he wanted ter do, but 'lustratin'--fer books and magazines, you know. She felt hurt, an' all put out at first: but Jimmy told her 'twas all right, an' that there was big money in it; so she got 'round contented again. She couldn't help it, anyhow, with Jimmy, he was that lovin' an' nice with her. He was the kind that's always bringin' footstools and shawls, an' makin' folks comfortable. Everybody loved Jimmy. Even the cats an' dogs rubbed up against him an' wagged their tails at sight of him, an' the kids--goodness, Jimmy couldn't cross the street without a dozen kids makin' a grand rush fer him.

"Well, time went on, an' Jimmy grew tall an' good lookin'. Then came the girl--an' she was a girl, too. 'Course, Jimmy, bein' as how he'd had all the frostin' there was goin' on everythin' so fur, carried out the same idea in girls, an' picked out the purtiest one he could find-- rich old Townsend's daughter, Bessie.

"To the Hadleys this seemed all right--Jimmy was merely gettin' the best, as usual; but the rest of us, includin' old man Townsend, begun ter sit up an' take notice. The old man was mad clean through. He had other plans fer Bessie, an' he said so purty plain."

"But it seems there didn't any of us--only Jimmy, maybe--take the girl herself into consideration. For a time she was a little skittish, an' led Jimmy a purty chase with her dancin' nearer an' nearer, an' then flyin' off out of reach. But at last she came out fair an' square fur Jimmy, an' they was as lively a pair of lovers as ye'd wish ter see. It looked, too, as if she'd even wheedle the old man 'round ter her side of thinkin'.'"

"The next thing we knew Jimmy had gone ter New York. He was ter study, an' at the same time pick up what work he could, ter turn an honest penny, the Hadleys said. We liked that in him. He was goin' ter make somethin' of himself, so's he'd be worthy of Bessie Townsend or any other girl."

"But't was hard on the Hadleys. Jimmy's lessons cost a lot, an' so did just livin' there in New York, an' 'course Jimmy couldn't pay fer it all, though I guess he worked nights an' Sundays ter piece out. Back home here the Hadleys scrimped an' scrimped till they didn't have half enough ter eat, an' hardly enough ter cover their nakedness. But they didn't mind--'t was fer Jimmy. He wrote often, an' told how he was workin', an' the girl got letters, too; at least, Mis' Hadley said she did. An' once in a while he'd tell of some picture he'd finished, or what the teacher said.

"But by an' by the letters didn't come so often. Sam told me about it at first, an' he said it plagued his wife a lot. He said she thought maybe Jimmy was gettin' discouraged, specially as he didn't seem ter say much of anything about his work now. Sam owned up that the letters wan't so free talkin'; an' that worried him. He was afraid the boy was keepin' back somethin'. He asked me, kind of sheepish-like, if I s'posed such a thing could be as that Jimmy had gone wrong, somehow. He knew cities was awful wicked an' temptin', he said.

"I laughed him out of that notion quick, an' I was honest in it, too. I'd have as soon suspected myself of goin' ter the bad as Jimmy, an' I told him so. Things didn't look right, though. The letters got skurser an' skurser, an' I began ter think myself maybe somethin' was up. Then come the newspaper.

"It was me that took it over to the Hadleys. It was a little notice in my weekly, an' I spied it 'way down in the corner just as I thought I had the paper all read. 'Twan't so much, but to us 'twas a powerful lot; jest a little notice that they was glad ter see that the first prize had gone ter the talented young illustrator, James Hadley, an' that he deserved it, an' they wished him luck.

"The Hadleys were purty pleased, you'd better believe. They hadn't seen it, 'course, as they wan't wastin' no money on weeklies them days. Sam set right down an' wrote, an' so did Mis' Hadley, right out of the fullness of their hearts. Mis' Hadley give me her letter ter read, she was that proud an' excited; an' 't was a good letter, all brimmin' over with love an' pride an' joy in his success. I could see just how Jimmy'd color up an' choke when he read it, specially where she owned up how she'd been gettin' purty near discouraged 'cause they didn't hear much from him, an' how she'd rather die than have her Jimmy fail.

"Well, they sent off the letters, an' by an' by come the answer. It was kind of shy and stiff-like, an' I think it sort of disappointed 'em; but they tried ter throw it off an' say that Jimmy was so modest he didn't like ter take praise.

"'Course the whole town was interested, an' proud, too, ter think he belonged ter us; an' we couldn't hear half enough about him. But as time went on we got worried. Things didn't look right. The Hadleys was still scrimpin', still sendin' money when they could, an' they owned up that Jimmy's letters wan't real satisfyin' an' that they didn't come often, though they always told how hard he was workin'.

"What was queerer still, every now an' then I'd see his name in my weekly. I looked fer it, I'll own. I run across it once in the 'Personals,' an' after that I hunted the paper all through every week. He went ter parties an' theaters, an' seemed ter be one of a gay crowd that was always havin' good times. I didn't say nothin' ter the Hadleys about all this, 'course, but it bothered me lots. What with all these fine doin's, an' his not sendin' any money home, it looked as if the old folks didn't count much now, an' that his head had got turned sure.

"As time passed, things got worse an' worse. Sam lost two cows, an' Mis' Hadley grew thinner an' whiter, an' finally got down sick in her bed. Then I wrote. I told Jimmy purty plain how things was an' what I thought of him. I told him that there wouldn't be any more money comin' from this direction (an' I meant ter see that there wan't, too!), an' I hinted that if that 'ere prize brought anythin' but honor, I should think 't would be a mighty good plan ter share it with the folks that helped him ter win it.

"It was a sharp letter, an' when it was gone I felt 'most sorry I'd sent it; an' when the answer come, I was sorry. Jimmy was all broke up, an' he showed it. He begged me ter tell him jest how his ma was; an' if they needed anythin', ter get it and call on him. He said he wished the prize had brought him lots of money, but it hadn't. He enclosed twenty-five dollars, however, and said he should write the folks not ter send him any more money, as he was goin' ter send it ter them now instead.

"Of course I took the letter an' the money right over ter Sam, an' after they'd got over frettin' 'cause I'd written at all, they took the money, an' I could see it made 'em look ten years younger. After that you couldn't come near either of 'em that you didn't hear how good Jimmy was an' how he was sendin' home money every week.

"Well, it wan't four months before I had ter write Jimmy again. Sam asked me too, this time. Mis' Hadley was sick again, an' Sam was worried. He thought Jimmy ought ter come home, but he didn't like ter say so himself. He wondered if I wouldn't drop him a hint. So I wrote, an' Jimmy wrote right away that he'd come.

"We was all of a twitter, 'course, then--the whole town. He'd got another prize--so the paper said--an' there was a paragraph praisin' up some pictures of his in the magazine. He was our Jimmy, an' we was proud of him, yet we couldn't help wonderin' how he'd act. We wan't used ter celebrities--not near to!

"Well, he came. He was taller an' thinner than when he went away, an' there was a tired look in his eyes that went straight ter my heart. 'Most the whole town was out ter meet him, an' that seemed ter bother him. He was cordial enough, in a way, but he seemed ter try ter avoid folks, an' he asked me right off ter get him 'out of it.' I could see he wan't hankerin' ter be made a lion of, so we got away soon's we could an' went ter his home.

"You should have seen Mis' Hadley's eyes when she saw him, tall an' straight in the doorway. And Sam--Sam cried like a baby, he was so proud of that boy. As fer Jimmy, his eyes jest shone, an' the tired look was all gone from them when he strode across the room an' dropped on his knees at his mother's bedside with a kind of choking cry. I come away then, and left them.

"We was kind of divided about Jimmy, after that. We liked him, 'most all of us, but we didn't like his ways. He was too stand-offish, an' queer, an' we was all mad at the way he treated the girl.

"'Twas given out that the engagement was broken, but we didn't believe 't was her done it, 'cause up ter the last minute she'd been runnin' down ter the house with posies and goodies. Then he came, an' she stopped. He didn't go there, neither, an', so far as we knew, they hadn't seen each other once. The whole town was put out. We didn't relish seein' her thrown off like an old glove, jest 'cause he was somebody out in the world now, an' could have his pick of girls with city airs and furbelows. But we couldn't do nothin', 'cause he he was good ter his folks, an' no mistake, an' we did like that.

"Mis' Hadley got better in a couple of weeks, an' he begun ter talk of goin' back. We wanted ter give him a banquet an' speeches and a serenade, but he wouldn't hear a word of it. He wouldn't let us tell him how pleased we was at his success, either. The one thing he wouldn't talk about was his work, an' some got most mad, he was so modest.

"He hardly ever left the house except fer long walks, and it was on one of them that the accident happened. It was in the road right in front of the field where I was ploughing, so I saw it all. Bessie Townsend, on her little gray mare, came tearin' down the Townsend Hill like mad.

"Jimmy had stopped ter speak ter me, at the fence, but the next minute he was off like a shot up the road. He ran an' made a flyin' leap, an' I saw the mare rear and plunge. Then beast and man came down together, and I saw Bessie slide to the ground, landin' on her feet.

"When I got there Bessie Townsend was sittin' on the ground, with Jimmy's head in her arms, which I thought uncommon good of her, seein' the mortification he'd caused her. But when I saw the look in her eyes, an' in his as he opened them an' gazed up at her, I reckoned there might be more ter that love-story than most folks knew. What he said ter her then I don't know, but ter me he said jest four words, 'Don't--tell--the--folks,' an' I didn't rightly understand jest then what he meant, for surely an accident like that couldn't be kept unbeknownst. The next minute he fell back unconscious.

"It was a bad business all around, an' from the very first there wan't no hope. In a week 'twas over, an' we laid poor Jimmy away. Two days after the funeral Sam come ter me with a letter. It was addressed ter Jimmy, an' the old man couldn't bring himself ter open it. He wanted, too, that I should go on ter New York an' get Jimmy's things; an' after I had opened the letter I said right off that I'd go. I was mad over that letter. It was a bill fer a suit of clothes, an' it asked him purty sharplike ter pay it.

"I had some trouble in New York findin' Jimmy's boardin'-place. There had been a fire the night before, an' his landlady had had ter move; but at last I found her an' asked anxiously fer Jimmy's things, an' if his pictures had been hurt.

"Jimmy's landlady was fat an' greasy an' foreign-lookin', an' she didn't seem ter understand what I was talkin' about till I repeated a bit sharply:--

"'Yes, his pictures. I've come fer 'em.'

"Then she shook her head.

"'Meester Hadley did not have any pictures.'

"'But he must have had 'em,' says I, 'fer them papers an' magazines he worked for. He made 'em!'

"She shook her head again; then she gave a queer hitch to her shoulders, and a little flourish with her hands.

"'Oh--ze pictures! He did do them--once--a leetle: months ago.'

"'But the prize,' says I. 'The prize ter James Hadley!'

"Then she laughed as if she suddenly understood.

"Oh, but it is ze grand mistake you are makin',' she cried, in her silly, outlandish way of talkin'. 'There is a Meester James Hadley, an' he does make pictures--beautiful pictures--but it is not this one. This Meester Hadley did try, long ago, but he failed to succeed, so my son said; an' he had to--to cease. For long time he has worked for me, for the grocer, for any one who would pay--till a leetle while ago. Then he left. In ze new clothes he had bought, he went away. Ze old ones-- burned. He had nothing else.'

"She said more, but I didn't even listen. I was back with Jimmy by the roadside, and his 'Don't--tell--the--folks' was ringin' in my ears. I understood it then, the whole thing from the beginnin'; an' I felt dazed an' shocked, as if some one had struck me a blow in the face. I wan't brought up ter think lyin' an' deceivin' was right.

"I got up by an' by an' left the house. I paid poor Jimmy's bill fer clothes--the clothes that I knew he wore when he stood tall an' straight in the doorway ter meet his mother's adorin' eyes. Then I went home.

"I told Sam that Jimmy's things got burned up in the fire--which was the truth. I stopped there. Then I went to see the girl--an' right there I got the surprise of my life. She knew. He had told her the whole thing long before he come home, an' insisted on givin' her up. Jest what he meant ter do in the end, an' how he meant ter do it, she didn't know; an' she said with a great sob in her voice, that she didn't believe he knew either. All he did know, apparently, was that he didn't mean his ma should find out an' grieve over it--how he had failed. But whatever he was goin' ter do, it was taken quite out of his hands at the last.

"As fer Bessie, now,--it seems as if she can't do enough fer Sam an' Mis' Hadley, she's that good ter 'em; an' they set the world by her. She's got a sad, proud look to her eyes, but Jimmy's secret is safe.

"As I said, I saw old Sam an' his wife in the cemetery to-night. They stopped me as usual, an' told me all over again what a good boy Jimmy was, an' how smart he was, an' what a lot he'd made of himself in the little time he'd lived. The Hadleys are old an' feeble an' broken, an' it's their one comfort--Jimmy's success."

Uncle Zeke paused, and drew a long breath. Then he eyed me almost defiantly.

"I ain't sayin' that Jimmy did right, of course; but I ain't sayin'-- that Jimmy did wrong," he finished.

ACROSS THE YEARS BY ELEANOR H. PORTER

A Summons Home

Mrs. Thaddeus Clayton came softly into the room and looked with apprehensive eyes upon the little old man in the rocking-chair.

"How be ye, dearie? Yer hain't wanted fer nothin', now, have ye?" she asked.

"Not a thing, Harriet," he returned cheerily. "I'm feelin' real pert, too. Was there lots there? An' did Parson Drew say a heap o' fine things?"

Mrs. Clayton dropped into a chair and pulled listlessly at the black strings of her bonnet.

"'T was a beautiful fun'ral, Thaddeus--a beautiful fun'ral. I--I 'most wished it was mine."

"Harriet!"

She gave a shamed-faced laugh.

"Well, I did--then Jehiel and Hannah Jane would 'a' come, an' I could 'a' seen 'em."

The horrified look on the old man's face gave way to a broad smile.

"Oh, Harriet--Harriet!" he chuckled, "how could ye seen 'em if you was dead?"

"Huh? Well, I--Thaddeus,"--her voice rose sharply in the silent room,-- "every single one of them Perkins boys was there, and Annabel, too. Only think what poor Mis' Perkins would 'a' given ter seen 'em 'fore she went! But they waited--waited, Thaddeus, jest as everybody does, till their folks is dead."

"But, Harriet," demurred the old man, "surely you'd 'a' had them boys come ter their own mother's fun'ral!"

"Come! I'd 'a' had 'em come before, while Ella Perkins could 'a' feasted her eyes on 'em. Thaddeus,"--Mrs. Clayton rose to her feet and stretched out two gaunt hands longingly,--"Thaddeus, I get so hungry sometimes for Jehiel and Hannah Jane, seems as though I jest couldn't stand it!"

"I know--I know, dearie," quavered the old man, vigorously polishing his glasses.

"Fifty years ago my first baby came," resumed the woman in tremulous tones; "then another came, and another, till I'd had six. I loved 'em, an' tended 'em, an' cared fer 'em, an' didn't have a thought but was fer them babies. Four died,"--her voice broke, then went on with renewed strength,--"but I've got Jehiel and Hannah Jane left; at least, I've got two bits of paper that comes mebbe once a month, an' one of 'em's signed 'your dutiful son, Jehiel,' an' the other, 'from your loving daughter, Hannah Jane.'"

"Well, Harriet, they--they're pretty good ter write letters," ventured Mr. Clayton.

"Letters!" wailed his wife. "I can't hug an' kiss letters, though I try to, sometimes. I want warm flesh an' blood in my arms, Thaddeus; I want ter look down into Jehiel's blue eyes an' hear him call me 'dear old mumsey!' as he used to. I wouldn't ask 'em ter stay--I ain't unreasonable, Thaddeus. I know they can't do that."

"Well, well, wife, mebbe they'll come--mebbe they'll come this summer; who knows?"

She shook her head dismally.

"You've said that ev'ry year for the last fifteen summers, an' they hain't come yet. Jehiel went West more than twenty years ago, an' he's never been home since. Why, Thaddeus, we've got a grandson 'most eighteen, that we hain't even seen! Hannah Jane's been home jest once since she was married, but that was nigh on ter sixteen years ago. She's always writin' of her Tommy and Nellie, but--I want ter see 'em, Thaddeus; I want ter see 'em!"

"Yes, yes; well, we'll ask 'em, Harriet, again--we'll ask 'em real urgent-like, an' mebbe that'll fetch 'em," comforted the old man. "We'll ask 'em ter be here the Fourth; that's eight weeks off yet, an' I shall be real smart by then."

Two letters that were certainly "urgent-like" left the New England farmhouse the next morning. One was addressed to a thriving Western city, the other to Chattanooga, Tennessee.

In course of time the answers came. Hannah Jane's appeared first, and was opened with shaking fingers.

Dear Mother [read Mrs. Clayton aloud]: Your letter came two or three days ago, and I have hurried round to answer it, for you seemed to be so anxious to hear. I'm real sorry, but I don't see how we can get away this summer. Nathan is real busy at the store; and, some way, I can't seem to get up energy enough to even think of fixing up the children to take them so far. Thank you for the invitation, though, and we should enjoy the visit very much; but I guess we can't go just yet. Of course if anything serious should come up that made it necessary-- why, that would be different: but I know you are sensible, and will understand how it is with us.

Nathan is well, but business has been pretty brisk, and he is in the store early and late. As long as he's making money, he don't mind; but I tell him I think he might rest a little sometimes, and let some one else do the things he does.

Tom is a big boy now, smart in his studies and with a good head for figures. Nellie loves her books, too; and, for a little girl of eleven, does pretty well, we think.

I must close now. We all send love, and hope you are getting along all right. Was glad to hear father was gaining so fast.

Your loving daughter

Hannah Jane

The letter dropped from Mrs. Clayton's fingers and lay unheeded on the floor. The woman covered her face with her hands and rocked her body back and forth.

"There, there, dearie," soothed the old man huskily; "mebbe Jehiel's will be diff'rent. I shouldn't wonder, now, if Jehiel would come. There, there! don't take on so, Harriet! don't! I jest know Jehiel'll come."

A week later Mrs. Clayton found another letter in the rural delivery box. She clutched it nervously, peered at the writing with her dim old eyes, and hurried into the house for her glasses.

Yes, it was from Jehiel.

She drew a long breath. Her eager thumb was almost under the flap of the envelope when she hesitated, eyed the letter uncertainly, and thrust it into the pocket of her calico gown. All day it lay there, save at times-- which, indeed, were of frequent occurrence-- when she took it from its hiding-place, pressed it to her cheek, or gloried in every curve of the boldly written address.

At night, after the lamp was lighted, she said to her husband in tones so low he could scarcely hear:

"Thaddeus, I--I had a letter from Jehiel to-day."

"You did--and never told me? Why, Harriet, what--" He paused helplessly.

"I--I haven't read it, Thaddeus," she stammered. "I couldn't bear to, someway. I don't know why, but I couldn't. You read it!" She held out the letter with shaking hands.

He took it, giving her a sharp glance from anxious eyes. As he began to read aloud she checked him.

"No; ter yerself, Thaddeus--ter yerself! Then--tell me."

As he read she watched his face. The light died from her eyes and her chin quivered as she saw the stern lines deepen around his mouth. A minute more, and he had finished the letter and laid it down without a word.

"Thaddeus, ye don't mean--he didn't say--"

"Read it--I--I can't," choked the old man.

She reached slowly for the sheet of paper and spread it on the table before her.

Dear Mother [Jehiel had written]: Just a word to tell you we are all O. K. and doing finely. Your letter reminded me that it was about time I was writing home to the old folks. I don't mean to let so many weeks go by without a letter from me, but somehow the time just gets away from me before I know it.

Minnie is well and deep in spring sewing and house-cleaning. I know-- because dressmaker's bills are beginning to come in, and every time I go home I find a carpet up in a new place!

Our boy Fred is eighteen to-morrow. You'd be proud of him, I know, if you could see him. Business is rushing. Glad to hear you're all right and that father's rheumatism is on the gain.

As ever, your affectionate and dutiful son, JEHIEL

Oh, by the way--about that visit East. I reckon we'll have to call it off this year. Too bad; but can't seem to see my way clear.

Bye-bye, J.

Harriet Clayton did not cry this time. She stared at the letter long minutes with wide-open, tearless eyes, then she slowly folded it and put it back in its envelope.

"Harriet, mebbe-" began the old man timidly.

"Don't, Thaddeus--please don't!" she interrupted. "I--I don't want ter talk." And she rose unsteadily to her feet and moved toward the kitchen door.

For a time Mrs. Clayton went about her work in a silence quite unusual, while her husband watched her with troubled eyes. His heart grieved over the bowed head and drooping shoulders, and over the blurred eyes that were so often surreptitiously wiped on a corner of the gingham apron. But at the end of a week the little old woman accosted him with a face full of aggressive yet anxious determination.

"Thaddeus, I want ter speak ter you about somethin'. I've been thinkin' it all out, an' I've decided that I've got ter kill one of us off."

"Harriet!"

"Well, I have. A fun'ral is the only thing that will fetch Jehiel and--"

"Harriet, are ye gone crazy? Have ye gone clean mad?"

She looked at him appealingly.

"Now, Thaddeus, don't try ter hender me, please. You see it's the only way. A fun'ral is the--"

"A 'fun'ral'--it's murder!" he shuddered.

"Oh, not ter make believe, as I shall," she protested eagerly. "It's--"

"Make believe!"

"Why, yes, of course. You'll have ter be the one ter do it, 'cause I'm goin' ter be the dead one, an'--"

"Harriet!"

"There, there, please, Thaddeus! I've jest got ter see Jehiel and Hannah Jane 'fore I die!"

"But--they--they'll come if--"

"No, they won't come. We've tried it over an' over again; you know we have. Hannah Jane herself said that if anythin' 'serious' came up it would be diff'rent. Well, I'm goin' ter have somethin' 'serious' come up!"

"But, Harriet--"

"Now, Thaddeus," begged the woman, almost crying, "you must help me, dear. I've thought it all out, an' it's easy as can be. I shan't tell any lies, of course. I cut my finger to-day, didn't I?"

"Why--yes--I believe so," he acknowledged dazedly; "but what has that to do--"

"That's the 'accident,' Thaddeus. You're ter send two telegrams at once-- one ter Jehiel, an' one ter Hannah Jane. The telegrams will say: 'Accident to your mother. Funeral Saturday afternoon. Come at once.' That's jest ten words."

The old man gasped. He could not speak.

"Now, that's all true, ain't it?" she asked anxiously. "The 'accident' is this cut. The 'fun'ral' is old Mis' Wentworth's. I heard ter-day that they couldn't have it until Saturday, so that'll give us plenty of time ter get the folks here. I needn't say whose fun'ral it is that's goin' ter be on Saturday, Thaddeus! I want yer ter hitch up an' drive over ter Hopkinsville ter send the telegrams. The man's new over there, an' won't know yer. You couldn't send 'em from here, of course."

Thaddeus Clayton never knew just how he allowed himself to be persuaded to take his part in this "crazy scheme," as he termed it, but persuaded he certainly was.

It was a miserable time for Thaddeus then. First there was that hurried drive to Hopkinsville. Though the day was warm he fairly shivered as he handed those two fateful telegrams to the man behind the counter. Then there was the homeward trip, during which, like the guilty thing he was, he cast furtive glances from side to side.

Even home itself came to be a misery, for the sweeping and the dusting and the baking and the brewing which he encountered there left him no place to call his own, so that he lost his patience at last and moaned:

"Seems ter me, Harriet, you're a pretty lively corpse!"

His wife smiled, and flushed a little.

"There, there, dear! don't fret. Jest think how glad we'll be ter see 'em!" she exclaimed.

Harriet was blissfully happy. Both the children had promptly responded to the telegrams, and were now on their way. Hannah Jane, with her husband and two children, were expected on Friday evening; but Jehiel and his wife and boy could not possibly get in until early on the following morning.

All this brought scant joy to Thaddeus. There was always hanging over him the dread horror of what he had done, and the fearful questioning as to how it was all going to end.

Friday came, but a telegram at the last moment told of trains delayed and connections missed. Hannah Jane would not reach home until nine-forty the next morning. So it was with a four-seated carryall that Thaddeus Clayton started for the station on Saturday morning to meet both of his children and their families.

The ride home was a silent one; but once inside the house, Jehiel and Hannah Jane, amid a storm of sobs and cries, besieged their father with questions.

The family were all in the darkened sitting-room--all, indeed, save Harriet, who sat in solitary state in the chamber above, her face pale and her heart beating almost to suffocation. It had been arranged that she was not to be seen until some sort of explanation had been given.

"Father, what was it?" sobbed Hannah Jane. "How did it happen?"

"It must have been so sudden," faltered Jehiel. "It cut me up completely."

"I can't ever forgive myself," moaned Hannah Jane hysterically. "She wanted us to come East, and I wouldn't. 'Twas my selfishness--'twas easier to stay where I was; and now--now--"

"We've been brutes, father," cut in Jehiel, with a shake in his voice; "all of us. I never thought--I never dreamed-father, can--can we see-- her?"

In the chamber above a woman sprang to her feet. Harriet had quite forgotten the stove-pipe hole to the room below, and every sob and moan and wailing cry had been woefully distinct to her ears. With streaming eyes and quivering lips she hurried down the stairs and threw open the sitting-room door.

"Jehiel! Hannah Jane! I'm here, right here--alive!" she cried. "An' I've been a wicked, wicked woman! I never thought how bad 'twas goin' ter make you feel. I truly never, never did. 'Twas only myself--I wanted yer so. Oh, children, children, I've been so wicked--so awful wicked!"

Jehiel and Hannah Jane were steady of head and strong of heartland joy, it is said, never kills; otherwise, the results of that sudden apparition in the sitting-room doorway might have been disastrous.

As it was, a wonderfully happy family party gathered around the table an hour later; and as Jehiel led a tremulous, gray-haired woman to the seat of honor, he looked into her shining eyes and whispered:

"Dear old mumsey, now that we've found the way home again, I reckon we'll be coming every year--don't you?"

The Black Silk Gowns

The Heath twins, Miss Priscilla and Miss Amelia, rose early that morning, and the world looked very beautiful to them--one does not buy a black silk gown every day; at least, Miss Priscilla and Miss Amelia did not. They had waited, indeed, quite forty years to buy this one.

The women of the Heath family had always possessed a black silk gown. It was a sort of outward symbol of inward respectability--an unfailing indicator of their proud position as members of one of the old families. It might be donned at any time after one's twenty-first birthday, and it should be donned always for funerals, church, and calls after one had turned thirty. Such had been the code of the Heath family for generations, as Miss Priscilla and Miss Amelia well knew; and it was this that had made all the harder their own fate--that their twenty-first birthday was now forty years behind them, and not yet had either of them attained this cachet of respectability.

To-day, however, there was to come a change. No longer need the carefully sponged and darned black alpaca gowns flaunt their wearers' poverty to the world, and no longer would they force these same wearers to seek dark corners and sunless rooms, lest the full extent of that poverty become known. It had taken forty years of the most rigid economy to save the necessary money; but it was saved now, and the dresses were to be bought. Long ago there had been enough for one, but neither of the women had so much as thought of the possibility of buying one silk gown. It was sometimes said in the town that if one of the Heath twins strained her eyes, the other one was obliged at once to put on glasses; and it is not to be supposed that two sisters whose sympathies were so delicately attuned would consent to appear clad one in new silk and the other in old alpaca.

In spite of their early rising that morning, it was quite ten o'clock before Miss Priscilla and Miss Amelia had brought the house into the state of speckless nicety that would not shame the lustrous things that were so soon to be sheltered beneath its roof. Not that either of the ladies expressed this sentiment in words, or even in their thoughts; they merely went about their work that morning with the reverent joy that a devoted priestess might feel in making ready a shrine for its idol. They had to hurry a little to get themselves ready for the eleven o'clock stage that passed their door; and they were still a little breathless when they boarded the train at the home station for the city twenty miles away--the city where were countless yards of shimmering silk waiting to be bought.

In the city that night at least six clerks went home with an unusual weariness in their arms, which came from lifting down and displaying almost their entire stock of black silk. But with all the weariness, there was no irritation; there was only in their nostrils a curious perfume as of lavender and old lace, and in their hearts a strange exaltation as if they had that day been allowed a glad part in a sacred rite. As for Miss Priscilla and Miss Amelia, they went home awed, yet triumphant: when one has waited forty years to make a purchase one does not make that purchase lightly.

"To-morrow we will go over to Mis' Snow's and see about having them made up," said Miss Priscilla with a sigh of content, as the stage lumbered through the dusty home streets.

"Yes; we want them rich, but plain," supplemented Miss Amelia, rapturously. "Dear me, Priscilla, but I am tired!"

In spite of their weariness the sisters did not get to bed very early that night. They could not decide whether the top drawer of the spare-room bureau or the long box in the parlor closet would be the safer refuge for their treasure. And when the matter was decided, and the sisters had gone to bed, Miss Priscilla, after a prolonged discussion, got up and moved the silk to the other place, only to slip out of bed later, after a much longer discussion, and put it back. Even then they did not sleep well: for the first time in their lives they knew the responsibility that comes with possessions; they feared-- burglars.

With the morning sun, however, came peace and joy. No moth nor rust nor thief had appeared, and the lustrous lengths of shimmering silk defied the sun itself to find spot or blemish.

"It looks even nicer than it did in the store, don't it?" murmured Miss Priscilla, ecstatically, as she hovered over the glistening folds that she had draped in riotous luxury across the chair-back.

"Yes,--oh, yes!" breathed Miss Amelia. "Now let's hurry with the work so we can go right down to Mis' Snow's."

"Black silk-black silk!" ticked the clock to Miss Priscilla washing dishes at the kitchen sink.

"You've got a black silk! You've got a black silk!" chirped the robins to Miss Amelia looking for weeds in the garden.

At ten o'clock the sisters left the house, each with a long brown parcel carefully borne in her arms. At noon--at noon the sisters were back again, still carrying the parcels. Their faces wore a look of mingled triumph and defeat.

"As if we could have that beautiful silk put into a plaited skirt!" quavered Miss Priscilla, thrusting the key into the lock with a trembling hand. "Why, Amelia, plaits always crack!"

"Of course they do!" almost sobbed Miss Amelia. "Only think of it, Priscilla, our silk--cracked!"

"We will just wait until the styles change," said Miss Priscilla, with an air of finality. "They won't always wear plaits!"

"And we know all the time that we've really got the dresses, only they aren't made up!" finished Miss Amelia, in tearful triumph.

So the silk was laid away in two big rolls, and for another year the old black alpaca gowns trailed across the town's thresholds and down the aisle of the church on Sunday. Their owners no longer sought shadowed corners and sunless rooms, however; it was not as if one were obliged to wear sponged and darned alpacas!

Plaits were "out" next year, and the Heath sisters were among the first to read it in the fashion notes. Once more on a bright spring morning Miss Priscilla and Miss Amelia left the house tenderly bearing in their arms the brown-paper parcels--and once more they returned, the brown parcels still in their arms. There was an air of indecision about them this time.

"You see, Amelia, it seemed foolish--almost wicked," Miss Priscilla was saying, "to put such a lot of that expensive silk into just sleeves."

"I know it," sighed her sister.

"Of course I want the dresses just as much as you do," went on Miss Priscilla, more confidently; "but when I thought of allowing Mis' Snow to slash into that beautiful silk and just waste it on those great balloon sleeves, I--I simply couldn't give my consent!-- and 'tisn't as though we hadn't got the dresses!"

"No, indeed!" agreed Miss Amelia, lifting her chin. And so once more the rolls of black silk were laid away in the great box that had already held them a year; and for another twelve months the black alpacas, now grown shabby indeed, were worn with all the pride of one whose garments are beyond reproach.

When for the third time Miss Priscilla and Miss Amelia returned to their home with the oblong brown parcels there was no indecision about them; there was only righteous scorn.

"And do you really think that Mis' Snow expected us to allow that silk to be cut up into those skimpy little skin-tight bags she called skirts?" demanded Miss Priscilla, in a shaking voice. "Why, Amelia, we couldn't ever make them over!"

"Of course we couldn't! And when skirts got bigger, what could we do?" cried Miss Amelia. "Why, I'd rather never have a black silk dress than to have one like that--that just couldn't be changed! We'll go on wearing the gowns we have. It isn't as if everybody didn't know we had these black silk dresses!"

When the fourth spring came the rolls of silk were not even taken from their box except to be examined with tender care and replaced in the enveloping paper. Miss Priscilla was not well. For weeks she had spent most of her waking hours on the sitting-room couch, growing thiner, weaker, and more hollow-eyed.

"You see, dear, I--I am not well enough now to wear it," she said faintly to her sister one day when they had been talking about the black silk gowns; "but you--" Miss Amelia had stopped her with a shocked gesture of the hand.

"Priscilla--as if I could!" she sobbed. And there the matter had ended.

The townspeople were grieved, but not surprised, when they learned that Miss Amelia was fast following her sister into a decline. It was what they had expected of the Heath twins, they said, and they reminded one another of the story of the strained eyes and the glasses. Then came the day when the little dressmaker's rooms were littered from end to end with black silk scraps.

"It's for Miss Priscilla and Miss Amelia,'" said Mrs. Snow, with tears in her eyes, in answer to the questions that were asked.

"It's their black silk gowns, you know."

"But I thought they were ill--almost dying!" gasped the questioner.

The little dressmaker nodded her head. Then she smiled, even while she brushed her eyes with her fingers.

"They are--but they're happy. They're even happy in this!" touching the dress in her lap. "They've been forty years buying it, and four making it up. Never until now could they decide to use it; never until now could they be sure they wouldn't want to--to make it--over." The little dressmaker's voice broke, then went on tremulously: "There are folks like that, you know--that never enjoy a thing for what it is, lest sometime they might want it--different. Miss Priscilla and Miss Amelia never took the good that was goin'; they've always saved it for sometime--later."

ACROSS THE YEARS BY ELEANOR H. PORTER

A Belated Honeymoon

The haze of a warm September day hung low over the house, the garden, and the dust-white road. On the side veranda a gray-haired, erect little figure sat knitting. After a time the needles began to move more and more slowly until at last they lay idle in the motionless, withered fingers.

"Well, well, Abby, takin' a nap?" demanded a thin-chested, wiry old man coming around the corner of the house and seating himself on the veranda steps.

The little old woman gave a guilty start and began to knit vigorously.

"Dear me, no, Hezekiah. I was thinkin'." She hesitated a moment, then added, a little feverishly: "--it's ever so much cooler here than up ter the fair grounds now, ain't it, Hezekiah?"

The old man threw a sharp look at her face. "Hm-m, yes," he said. "Mebbe 't is."

From far down the road came the clang of a bell. As by common consent the old man and his wife got to their feet and hurried to the front of the house where they could best see the trolley-car as it rounded a curve and crossed the road at right angles.

"Goes slick, don't it?" murmured the man.

There was no answer. The woman's eyes were hungrily devouring the last glimpse of paint and polish.

"An' we hain't been on 'em 't all yet, have we, Abby?" he continued.

She drew a long breath.

"Well, ye see, I--I hain't had time, Hezekiah," she rejoined apologetically.

"Humph!" muttered the old man as they turned and walked back to their seats.

For a time neither spoke, then Hezekiah Warden cleared his throat determinedly and faced his wife.

"Look a' here, Abby," he began, "I'm agoin' ter say somethin' that has been 'most tumblin' off'n the end of my tongue fer mor'n a year. Jennie an' Frank are good an' kind an' they mean well, but they think 'cause our hair's white an' our feet ain't quite so lively as they once was, that we're jest as good as buried already, an' that we don't need anythin' more excitin' than a nap in the sun. Now, Abby, didn't ye want ter go ter that fair with the folks ter-day? Didn't ye?"

A swift flush came into the woman's cheek.

"Why, Hezekiah, it's ever so much cooler here, an'--" she paused helplessly.

"Humph!" retorted the man, "I thought as much. It's always 'nice an' cool' here in summer an' 'nice an' warm' here in winter when Jennie goes somewheres that you want ter go an' don't take ye. An' when 't ain't that, you say you 'hain't had time.' I know ye! You'd talk any way ter hide their selfishness. Look a' here, Abby, did ye ever ride in them 'lectric-cars? I mean anywheres?"

"Well, I hain't neither, an', by ginger, I'm agoin' to!"

"Oh, Hezekiah, Hezekiah, don't--swear!"

"I tell ye, Abby, I will swear. It's a swearin' matter. Ever since I heard of 'em I wanted ter try 'em. An' here they are now 'most ter my own door an' I hain't even been in 'em once. Look a' here, Abby, jest because we're 'most eighty ain't no sign we've lost int'rest in things. I'm spry as a cricket, an' so be you, yet Frank an' Jennie expect us ter stay cooped up here as if we was old--really old, ninety or a hundred, ye know--an' 't ain't fair. Why, we will be old one of these days!"

"I know it, Hezekiah."

"We couldn't go much when we was younger," he resumed. "Even our weddin' trip was chopped right off short 'fore it even begun."

A tender light came into the dim old eyes opposite.

"I know, dear, an' what plans we had!" cried Abigail; "Boston, an' Bunker Hill, an' Faneuil Hall."

The old man suddenly squared his shoulders and threw back his head.

"Abby, look a' here! Do ye remember that money I've been savin' off an' on when I could git a dollar here an' there that was extra? Well, there's as much as ten of 'em now, an' I'm agoin' ter spend 'em--all of 'em mebbe. I'm agoin' ter ride in them 'lectric-cars, an' so be you. An' I ain't goin' ter no old country fair, neither, an' no more be you. Look a' here, Abby, the folks are goin' again ter-morrer ter the fair, ain't they?"

Abigail nodded mutely. Her eyes were beginning to shine.

"Well," resumed Hezekiah, "when they go we'll be settin' in the sun where they say we'd oughter be. But we ain't agoin' ter stay there, Abby. We're goin' down the road an' git on them 'lectric-cars, an' when we git ter the Junction we're agoin' ter take the steam cars fer Boston. What if 'tis thirty miles! I calc'late we're equal to 'em. We'll have one good time, an' we won't come home until in the evenin'. We'll see Faneuil Hall an' Bunker Hill, an' you shall buy a new cap, an' ride in the subway. If there's a preachin' service we'll go ter that. They have 'em sometimes weekdays, ye know."

"Oh, Hezekiah, we--couldn't!" gasped the little old woman.

"Pooh! 'Course we could. Listen!" And Hezekiah proceeded to unfold his plans more in detail.

It was very early the next morning when the household awoke. By seven o'clock a two-seated carryall was drawn up to the side-door, and by a quarter past the carryall, bearing Jennie, Frank, the boys, and the lunch baskets, rumbled out of the yard and on to the highway.

"Now, keep quiet and don't get heated, mother," cautioned Jennie, looking back at the little gray-haired woman standing all alone on the side veranda.

"Find a good cool spot to smoke your pipe in, father," called Frank, as an old man appeared in the doorway.

There followed a shout, a clatter, and a cloud of dust--then silence. Fifteen minutes later, hand in hand, a little old man and a little old woman walked down the white road together.

To most of the passengers on the trolley-car that day the trip was merely a necessary means to an end; to the old couple on the front seat it was something to be remembered and lived over all their lives. Even at the Junction the spell of unreality was so potent that the man forgot things so trivial as tickets, and marched into the car with head erect and eyes fixed straight ahead.

It was after Hezekiah had taken out the roll of bills--all ones--to pay the fares to the conductor that a young man in a tall hat sauntered down the aisle and dropped into the seat in front.

"Going to Boston, I take it," said the young man genially.

"Yes, sir," replied Hezehiah, no less genially. "Ye guessed right the first time."

Abigail lifted a cautious hand to her hair and her bonnet. So handsome and well-dressed a man would notice the slightest thing awry, she thought.

"Hm-m," smiled the stranger. "I was so successful that time, suppose I try my luck again.--You don't go every day, I fancy, eh?"

"Sugar! How'd he know that, now?" chuckled Hezekiah, turning to his wife in open glee. "So we don't, stranger, so we don't," he added, turning back to the man. "Ye hit it plumb right."

"Hm-m! great place, Boston," observed the stranger. "I'm glad you're going. I think you'll enjoy it."

The two wrinkled old faces before him fairly beamed.

"I thank ye, sir," said Hezekiah heartily. "I call that mighty kind of ye, specially as there are them that thinks we're too old ter be enj'yin' of anythin'."

"Old? Of course you're not too old! Why, you're just in the prime to enjoy things," cried the handsome man, and in the sunshine of his dazzling smile the hearts of the little old man and woman quite melted within them.

"Thank ye, sir, thank ye sir," nodded Abigail, while Hezekiah offered his hand.

"Shake, stranger, shake! An' I ain't too old, an' I'm agoin' ter prove it. I've got money, sir, heaps of it, an' I'm goin' ter spend it--mebbe I'll spend it all. We're agoin' ter see Bunker Hill an' Faneuil Hall, an' we're agoin' ter ride in the subway. Now, don't tell me we don't know how ter enj'y ourselves!"

It was a very simple matter after that. On the one hand were infinite tact and skill; on the other, innocence, ignorance, and an overwhelming gratitude for this sympathetic companionship.

Long before Boston was reached Mr. and Mrs. Warden and "Mr. Livingstone" were on the best of terms, and when they separated at the foot of the car-steps, to the old man and woman it seemed that half their joy and all their courage went with the smiling man who lifted his hat in farewell before being lost to sight in the crowd.

"There, Abby, we're here!" announced Hezekiah with an exultation that was a little forced. "Gorry! There must be somethin' goin' on ter-day," he added, as he followed the long line of people down the narrow passage between the cars.

There was no reply. Abigail's cheeks were pink and her bonnet-strings untied. Her eyes, wide opened and frightened, were fixed on the swaying, bobbing crowds ahead. In the great waiting-room she caught her husband's arm.

"Hezekiah, we can't, we mustn't ter-day," she whispered. "There's such a crowd. Let's go home an' come when it's quieter."

"But, Abby, we--here, let's set down," Hezekiah finished helplessly.

Near one of the outer doors Mr. Livingstone--better known to his friends and the police as "Slick Bill"--smiled behind his hand. Not once since he had left them had Mr. and Mrs. Hezekiah Warden been out of his sight.

"What's up, Bill? Need assistance?" demanded a voice at his elbow.

"Jim, by all that's lucky!" cried Livingstone, turning to greet a dapper little man in gray. "Sure I need you! It's a peach, though I doubt if we get much but fun, but there'll be enough of that to make up. Oh, he's got money--'heaps of it,' he says," laughed Livingstone, "and I saw a roll of bills myself. But I advise you not to count too much on that, though it'll be easy enough to get what there is, all right. As for the fun, Jim, look over by that post near the parcel window."

"Great Scott! Where'd you pick 'em?" chuckled the younger man.

"Never mind," returned the other with a shrug. "Meet me at Clyde's in half an hour. We'll be there, never fear."

Over by the parcel-room an old man looked about him with anxious eyes.

"But, Abby, don't ye see?" he urged. "We've come so fer, seems as though we oughter do the rest all right. Now, you jest set here an' let me go an' find out how ter git there. We'll try fer Bunker Hill first, 'cause we want ter see the munurmunt sure."

He rose to his feet only to be pulled back by his wife.

"Hezekiah Warden!" she almost sobbed. "If you dare ter stir ten feet away from me I'll never furgive ye as long as I live. We'd never find each other ag'in!"

"Well, well, Abby," soothed the man with grim humor, "if we never found each other ag'in, I don't see as 'twould make much diff'rence whether ye furgived me or not!"

For another long minute they silently watched the crowd. Then Hezekiah squared his shoulders.

"Come, come, Abby," he said, "this ain't no way ter do. Only think how we wanted ter git here an' now we're here an' don't dare ter stir. There ain't any less folks than there was-- growin' worse, if anythin'--but I'm gittin' used ter 'em now, an' I'm goin' ter make a break. Come, what would Mr. Livin'stone say if he could see us now? Where'd he think our boastin' was about our bein' able ter enj'y ourselves? Come!" And once more he rose to his feet.

This time he was not held back. The little woman at his side adjusted her bonnet, tilted up her chin, and in her turn rose to her feet.

"Sure enough!" she quavered bravely. "Come, Hezekiah, we'll ask the way ter Bunker Hill." And, holding fast to her husband's coat sleeve, she tripped across the floor to one of the outer doors.

On the sidewalk Mr. and Mrs. Hezekiah Warden came once more to a halt. Before them swept an endless stream of cars, carriages, and people. Above thundered the elevated railway cars.

"Oh-h," shuddered Abigail and tightened her grasp on her husband's coat.

It was some minutes before Hezekiah's dry tongue and lips could frame his question, and then his words were so low-spoken and indistinct that the first two men he asked did not hear. The third man frowned and pointed to a policeman. The fourth snapped: "Take the elevated for Charlestown or the trolley-cars, either;" all of which served but to puzzle Hezekiah the more.

Little by little the dazed old man and his wife fell back before the jostling crowds. They were quite against the side of the building when Livingstone spoke to them.

"Well, well, if here aren't my friends again!" he exclaimed cordially.

There was something of the fierceness of a drowning man in the way Hezekiah took hold of that hand.

"Mr. Livin'stone!" he cried; then he recollected himself. "We was jest goin' ter Bunker Hill," he said jauntily.

"Yes?" smiled Livingstone. "But your luncheon--aren't you hungry? Come with me; I was just going to get mine."

"But you--I--" Hezekiah paused and looked doubtingly at his wife.

"Indeed, my dear Mrs. Warden, you'll say 'Yes,' I know," urged Livingstone suavely. "Only think how good a nice cup of tea would taste now."

"I know, but--" She glanced at her husband.

"Nonsense! Of course you'll come," insisted Livingstone, laying a gently compelling hand on the arm of each.

Fifteen minutes later Hezekiah stood looking about him with wondering eyes.

"Well, well, Abby, ain't this slick?" he cried.

His wife did not reply. The mirrors, the lights, the gleaming silver and glass had filled her with a delight too great for words. She was vaguely conscious of her husband, of Mr. Livingstone, and of a smooth-shaven little man in gray who was presented as "Mr. Harding." Then she found herself seated at that wonderful table, while beside her chair stood an awesome being who laid a printed card before her. With a little ecstatic sigh she gave Hezekiah her customary signal for the blessing and bowed her head.

"There!" exulted Livingstone aloud. "Here we--" He stopped short. From his left came a deep-toned, reverent voice invoking the divine blessing upon the place, the food, and the new friends who were so kind to strangers in a strange land.

"By Jove!" muttered Livingstone under his breath, as his eyes met those of Jim across the table. The waiter coughed and turned his back. Then, the blessing concluded, Hezekiah raised his head and smiled.

"Well, well, Abby, why don't ye say somethin'?" he asked, breaking the silence. "Ye hain't said a word. Mr. Livin'stone'll be thinkin' ye don't like it."

Mrs. Warden drew a long breath of delight.

"I can't say anythin', Hezekiah," she faltered. "It's all so beautiful."

Livingstone waited until the dazed old eyes had become in a measure accustomed to the surroundings, then he turned a smiling face on Hezekiah.

"And now, my friend, what do you propose to do after luncheon?" he asked.

"Well, we cal'late ter take in Bunker Hill an' Faneuil Hall sure," returned the old man with a confidence that told of new courage imbibed with his tea. "Then we thought mebbe we'd ride in the subway an' hear one of the big preachers if they happened ter be holdin' meetin's anywheres this week. Mebbe you can tell us, eh?"

Across the table the man called Harding choked over his food and Livingstone frowned.

"Well," began Livingstone slowly.

"I think," interrupted Harding, taking a newspaper from his pocket, "I think there are services there," he finished gravely, pointing to the glaring advertisement of a ten-cent show, as he handed the paper across to Livingstone.

"But what time do the exercises begin?" demanded Hezekiah in a troubled voice. "Ye see, there's Bunker Hill an'--sugar! Abby, ain't that pretty?" he broke off delightedly. Before him stood a slender glass into which the waiter was pouring something red and sparkling.

The old lady opposite grew white, then pink. "Of course that ain't wine, Mr. Livingstone?" she asked anxiously.

"Give yourself no uneasiness, my dear Mrs. Warden," interposed Harding. "It's lemonade--pink lemonade."

"Oh," she returned with a relieved sigh. "I ask yer pardon, I'm sure. You wouldn't have it, 'course, no more'n I would. But, ye see, bein' pledged so, I didn't want ter make a mistake."

There was an awkward silence, then Harding raised his glass.

"Here's to your health, Mrs. Warden!" he cried gayly. "May your trip----"

"Wait!" she interrupted excitedly, her old eyes alight and her cheeks flushed. "Let me tell ye first what this trip is ter us, then ye'll have a right ter wish us good luck."

Harding lowered his glass and turned upon her a gravely attentive face.

"'Most fifty years ago we was married, Hezekiah an' me," she began softly. "We'd saved, both of us, an' we'd planned a honeymoon trip. We was comin' ter Boston. They didn't have any 'lectric-cars then nor any steam-cars only half-way. But we was comin' an' we was plannin' on Bunker Hill an' Faneuil Hall, an' I don't know what all."

The little lady paused for breath and Harding stirred uneasily in his chair. Livingstone did not move. His eyes were fixed on a mirror across the room. Over at the sideboard the waiter vigorously wiped a bottle.

"Well, we was married," continued the tremulous voice, "an' not half an hour later mother fell down the cellar stairs an' broke her hip. Of course that stopped things right short. I took off my weddin' gown an' put on my old red caliker an' went ter work. Hezekiah came right there an' run the farm an' I nursed mother an' did the work. 'T was more'n a year 'fore she was up 'round, an' after that, what with the babies an' all, there didn't never seem a chance when Hezekiah an' me could take this trip.

"If we went anywhere we couldn't seem ter manage ter go tergether, an' we never stayed fer no sight-seein'. Late years my Jennie an' her husband seemed ter think we didn't need nothin' but naps an' knittin', an' somehow we got so we jest couldn't stand it. We wanted ter go somewhere an' see somethin', so."

Mrs. Warden paused, drew a long breath, and resumed. Her voice now had a ring of triumph.

"Well, last month they got the 'lectric-cars finished down our way. We hadn't been on 'em, neither of us. Jennie an' Frank didn't seem ter want us to. They said they was shaky an' noisy an' would tire us all out. But yesterday, when the folks was gone, Hezekiah an' me got ter talkin' an' thinkin' how all these years we hadn't never had that honeymoon trip, an' how by an' by we'd be old--real old, I mean, so's we couldn't take it--an' all of a sudden we said we'd take it now, right now. An' we did. We left a note fer the children, an'--an' we're here!"

There was a long silence. Over at the sideboard the waiter still polished his bottle. Livingstone did not even turn his head. Finally Harding raised his glass.

"We'll drink to honeymoon trips in general and to this one in particular," he cried, a little constrainedly.

Mrs. Warden flushed, smiled, and reached for her glass. The pink lemonade was almost at her lips when Livingstone's arm shot out. Then came the tinkle of shattered glass and a crimson stain where the wine trailed across the damask.

"I beg your pardon!" exclaimed Livingstone, while the other men lowered their glasses in surprise. "That was an awkward slip of mine, Mrs. Warden. I must have hit your arm."

"But, Bill," muttered Harding under his breath, "you don't mean--"

"But I do," corrected Livingstone quietly, looking straight into Harding's amazed eyes.

"Mr. and Mrs. Warden are my guests. They are going to drive to Bunker Hill with me by and by."

When the six o'clock accommodation train pulled out from Boston that night it bore a little old man and a little old woman, gray-haired, weary, but blissfully content.

"We've seen 'em all, Hezekiah, ev'ry single one of 'em," Abigail was saying. "An' wan't Mr. Livingstone good, a-gittin' that carriage an' takin' us ev'rywhere; an' it bein' open so all 'round the sides, we didn't miss seein' a single thing!"

"He was, Abby, he was, an' he wouldn't let me pay one cent!" cried Hezekiah, taking out his roll of bills and patting it lovingly. "But, Abby, did ye notice? 'Twas kind o' queer we never got one taste of that pink lemonade. The waiter-man took it away."

When Aunt Abby Waked Up

The room was very still. The gaunt figure on the bed lay motionless save for a slight lifting of the chest at long intervals. The face was turned toward the wall, leaving a trail of thin gray hair-wisps across the pillow. Just outside the door two physicians talked together in low tones, with an occasional troubled glance toward the silent figure on the bed.

"If there could be something that would rouse her," murmured one; "something that would prick her will-power and goad it into action! But this lethargy--this wholesale giving up!" he finished with a gesture of despair.

"I know," frowned the other; "and I've tried--day after day I've tried. But there's nothing. I've exhausted every means in my power. I didn't know but you--" He paused questioningly.

The younger man shook his head.

"No," he said. "If you can't, I can't. You've been her physician for years. If anyone knows how to reach her, you should know. I suppose you've thought of--her son?"

"Oh, yes. Jed was sent for long ago, but he had gone somewhere into the interior on a prospecting trip, and was very hard to reach. It is doubtful if word gets to him at all until--too late. As you know, perhaps, it is rather an unfortunate case. He has not been home for years, anyway, and the Nortons--James is Mrs. Darling's nephew--have been making all the capital they can out of it, and have been prejudicing her against him-- quite unjustly, in my opinion, for I think it's nothing more nor less than thoughtlessness on the boy's part."

"Hm-m; too bad, too bad!" murmured the other, as he turned and led the way to the street door.

Back in the sick-room the old woman still lay motionless on the bed. She was wondering--as she had wondered so often before--why it took so long to die. For days now she had been trying to die, decently and in order. There was really no particular use in living, so far as she could see. Ella and Jim were very kind; but, after all, they were not Jed, and Jed was away--hopelessly away. He did not even want to come back, so Ella and Jim said.

There was the money, too. She did not like to think of the money. It seemed to her that every nickel and dime and quarter that she had painfully wrested from the cost of keeping soul and body together all these past years lay now on her breast with a weight that crushed like lead. She had meant that money for Jed. Ella and Jim were kind, of course, and she was willing they should have it; yet Jed--but Jed was away.

And she was so tired. She had ceased to rouse herself, either for the medicine or for the watery broths they forced through her lips. It was so hopelessly dragged out--this dying; yet it must be over soon. She had heard them tell the neighbors only yesterday that she was unconscious and that she did not know a thing of what was passing around her; and she had smiled--but only in her mind. Her lips, she knew, had not moved.

They were talking now--Ella and Jim--out in the other room. Their voices, even their words, were quite distinct, and dreamily, indifferently, she listened.

"You see," said Jim, "as long as I've got ter go ter town ter-morrer, anyhow, it seems a pity not ter do it all up at once. I could order the coffin an' the undertaker--it's only a question of a few hours, anyway, an' it seems such a pity ter make another trip--jest fer that!"

In the bedroom the old woman stirred suddenly. Somewhere, away back behind the consciousness of things, something snapped, and sent the blood tingling from toes to fingertips. A fierce anger sprang instantly into life and brushed the cobwebs of lethargy and indifference from her brain. She turned and opened her eyes, fixing them upon the oblong patch of light that marked the doorway leading to the room beyond where sat Ella and Jim.

"Jest fer that," Jim had said, and "that" was her death. It was not worth, it seemed, even an extra trip to town! And she had done so much-- so much for those two out there!

"Let's see; ter-day's Monday," Jim went on. "We might fix the fun'ral for Saturday, I guess, an' I'll tell the folks at the store ter spread it. Puttin' it on Sat'day'll give us a leetle extry time if she shouldn't happen ter go soon's we expect--though there ain't much fear o' that now, I guess, she's so low. An' it'll save me 'most half a day ter do it all up this trip. I ain't--what's that?" he broke off sharply.

From the inner room had seemed to come a choking, inarticulate cry.

With a smothered ejaculation Jim picked up the lamp, hurried into the sick-room, and tiptoed to the bed. The gaunt figure lay motionless, face to the wall, leaving a trail of thin gray hair-wisps across the pillow.

"Gosh!" muttered the man as he turned away.

"There's nothin' doin'-but it did give me a start!"

On the bed the woman smiled grimly--but the man did not see it.

It was snowing hard when Jim got back from town Tuesday night. He came blustering into the kitchen with stamping feet and wide-flung arms, scattering the powdery whiteness in all directions.

"Whew! It's a reg'lar blizzard," he began, but he stopped short at the expression on his wife's face. "Why, Ella!" he cried.

"Jim--Aunt Abby sat up ten minutes in bed ter-day. She called fer toast an' tea."

Jim dropped into a chair. His jaw fell open.

"S-sat up!" he stammered.

"Yes."

"But she--hang it all, Herrick's comin' ter-morrer with the coffin!"

"Oh, Jim!"

"Well, I can't help it! You know how she was this mornin'," retorted Jim sharply. "I thought she was dead once. Why, I 'most had Herrick come back with me ter-night, I was so sure."

"I know it," shivered Ella, "but you hadn't been gone an hour 'fore she began to stir an' notice things. I found her lookin' at me first, an' it give me such a turn I 'most dropped the medicine bottle in my hand. I was clearin' off the little table by her bed, an' she was followin' me around with them big gray eyes. 'Slickin' up?' she asks after a minute; an' I could 'a' dropped right there an' then, 'cause I was slickin' up, fer her fun'ral. 'Where's Jim?' she asks then. 'Gone ter town,' says I, kind o' faint-like. 'Umph!' she says, an' snaps her lips tight shet. After a minute she opens 'em again. 'I think I'll have some tea and toast,' she says, casual-like, jest as if she'd been callin' fer victuals ev'ry day fer a month past. An' when I brought it, if she didn't drag herself up in bed an' call fer a piller to her back, so's she could set up. An' there she stayed, pantin' an' gaspin', but settin' up--an' she stayed there till the toast an' tea was gone."

"Gosh!" groaned Jim. "Who'd 'a' thought it? 'Course 't ain't that I grudge the old lady's livin'," he added hurriedly, "but jest now it's so-- unhandy, things bein' as they be. We can't very well--" He stopped, a swift change coming to his face. "Say, Ella," he cried, "mebbe it's jest a spurt 'fore--'fore the last. Don't it happen sometimes that way--when folks is dyin'?"

"I don't know," shuddered Ella. "Sh-h! I thought I heard her." And she hurried across the hall to the sitting-room and the bedroom beyond.

It did not snow much through the night, but in the early morning it began again with increased severity. The wind rose, too, and by the time Herrick, the undertaker, drove into the yard, the storm had become a blizzard.

"I calc'lated if I didn't git this 'ere coffin here purty quick there wouldn't be no gettin' it here yet awhile," called Herrick cheerfully, as Jim came to the door.

Jim flushed and raised a warning hand.

"Sh-h! Herrick, look out!" he whispered hoarsely. "She ain't dead yet. You'll have ter go back."

"Go back!" snorted Herrick. "Why, man alive, 'twas as much as my life's worth to get here. There won't be no goin' back yet awhile fer me nor no one else, I calc'late. An' the quicker you get this 'ere coffin in out of the snow, the better't will be," he went on authoritatively as he leaped to the ground.

It was not without talk and a great deal of commotion that the untimely addition to James Norton's household effects was finally deposited in the darkened parlor; neither was it accomplished without some echo of the confusion reaching the sick-room, despite all efforts of concealment. Jim, perspiring, red-faced, and palpably nervous, was passing on tiptoe through the sitting-room when a quavering voice from the bedroom brought him to a halt.

"Jim, is that you?"

"Yes, Aunt Abby."

"Who's come?"

Jim's face grew white, then red.

"C-ome?" he stammered.

"Yes, I heard a sleigh and voices. Who is it?"

"Why, jest-jest a man on--on business," he flung over his shoulder, as he fled through the hall.

Not half an hour later came Ella's turn. In accordance with the sick woman's orders she had prepared tea, toast, and a boiled egg; but she had not set the tray on the bed when the old woman turned upon her two keen eyes.

"Who's in the kitchen, Ella, with Jim?"

Ella started guiltily.

"Why, jest a--a man."

"Who is it?"

Ella hesitated; then, knowing that deceit was useless, she stammered out the truth.

"Why, er--only Mr. Herrick."

"Not William Herrick, the undertaker!" There was apparently only pleased surprise in the old woman's voice.

"Yes," nodded Ella feverishly, "he had business out this way, and--and got snowed up," she explained with some haste.

"Ye don't say," murmured the old woman. "Well, ask him in; I'd like ter see him."

"Aunt Abby!"--Ella's teeth fairly chattered with dismay.

"Yes, I'd like ter see him," repeated the old woman with cordial interest. "Call him in."

And Ella could do nothing but obey.

Herrick, however, did not stay long in the sick-room. The situation was uncommon for him, and not without its difficulties. As soon as possible he fled to the kitchen, telling Jim that it gave him "the creeps" to have her ask him where he'd started for, and if business was good.

All that day it snowed and all that night; nor did the dawn of Friday bring clear skies. For hours the wind had swept the snow from roofs and hilltops, piling it into great drifts that grew moment by moment deeper and more impassable.

In the farmhouse Herrick was still a prisoner.

The sick woman was better. Even Jim knew now that it was no momentary flare of the candle before it went out. Mrs. Darling was undeniably improving in health. She had sat up several times in bed, and had begun to talk of wrappers and slippers. She ate toast, eggs, and jellies, and hinted at chicken and beefsteak. She was weak, to be sure, but behind her, supporting and encouraging, there seemed to be a curious strength--a strength that sent a determined gleam to her eyes, and a grim tenseness to her lips.

At noon the sun came out, and the wind died into fitful gusts. The two men attacked the drifts with a will, and made a path to the gate. They even attempted to break out the road, and Herrick harnessed his horse and started for home; but he had not gone ten rods before he was forced to turn back.

"'T ain't no use," he grumbled. "I calc'late I'm booked here till the crack o' doom!"

"An' ter-morrer's the fun'ral," groaned Jim. "An' I can't git nowhere--nowhere ter tell 'em not ter come!"

"Well, it don't look now as if anybody'd come--or go," snapped the undertaker.

Saturday dawned fair and cold. Early in the morning the casket was moved from the parlor to the attic.

There had been sharp words at the breakfast table, Herrick declaring that he had made a sale, and refusing to take the casket back to town; hence the move to the attic; but in spite of their caution, the sick woman heard the commotion.

"What ye been cartin' upstairs?" she asked in a mildly curious voice.

Ella was ready for her.

"A chair," she explained smoothly; "the one that was broke in the front room, ye know." And she did not think it was necessary to add that the chair was not all that had been moved. She winced and changed color, however, when her aunt observed:

"Humph! Must be you're expectin' company, Ella."

It was almost two o'clock when loud voices and the crunch of heavy teams told that the road-breakers had come. All morning the Nortons had been hoping against hope that the fateful hour would pass, and the road be still left in unbroken whiteness. Someone, however, had known his duty too well--and had done it.

"I set ter work first thing on this road," said the man triumphantly to Ella as he stood, shovel in hand, at the door. "The parson's right behind, an' there's a lot more behind him. Gorry! I was afraid I wouldn't git here in time, but the fun'ral wan't till two, was it?"

Ella's dry lips refused to move. She shook her head.

"There's a mistake," she said faintly. "There ain't no fun'ral. Aunt Abby's better."

The man stared, then he whistled softly.

"Gorry!" he muttered, as he turned away.

If Jim and Ella had supposed that they could keep their aunt from attending her own "funeral"--as Herrick persisted in calling it--they soon found their mistake. Mrs. Darling heard the bells of the first arrival.

"I guess mebbe I'll git up an' set up a spell," she announced calmly to Ella. "I'll have my wrapper an' my slippers, an' I'll set in the big chair out in the settin'-room. That's Parson Gerry's voice, an' I want ter see him."

"But, Aunt Abby--" began Ella, feverishly.

"Well, I declare, if there ain't another sleigh drivin' in," cried the old woman excitedly, sitting up in bed and peering through the little window. "Must be they're givin' us a s'prise party. Now hurry, Ella, an' git them slippers. I ain't a-goin' to lose none o' the fun!" And Ella, nervous, perplexed, and thoroughly frightened, did as she was bid.

In state, in the big rocking-chair, the old woman received her guests. She said little, it is true, but she was there; and if she noticed that no guest entered the room without a few whispered words from Ella in the hall, she made no sign. Neither did she apparently consider it strange that ten women and six men should have braved the cold to spend fifteen rather embarrassed minutes in her sitting-room--and for this last both Ella and Jim were devoutly grateful. They could not help wondering about it, however, after she had gone to bed, and the house was still.

"What do ye s'pose she thought?" whispered Jim.

"I don't know," shivered Ella, "but, Jim, wan't it awful?--Mis' Blair brought a white wreath--everlastin's!"

One by one the days passed, and Jim and Ella ceased to tremble every time the old woman opened her lips. There was still that fearsome thing in the attic, but the chance of discovery was small now.

"If she should find out," Ella had said, "'twould be the end of the money--fer us."

"But she ain't a-goin' ter find out," Jim had retorted. "She can't last long, 'course, an' I guess she won't change the will now--unless some one tells her; an' I'll be plaguy careful there don't no one do that!"

The "funeral" was a week old when Mrs. Darling came into the sitting-room one day, fully dressed.

"I put on all my clo's," she said smilingly, in answer to Ella's shocked exclamation. "I got restless, somehow, an' sick o' wrappers. Besides, I wanted to walk around the house a little. I git kind o' tired o' jest one room." And she limped across the floor to the hall door.

"But, Aunt Abby, where ye goin' now?" faltered Ella.

"Jest up in the attic. I wanted ter see--" She stopped in apparent surprise. Ella and Jim had sprung to their feet.

"The attic!" they gasped.

"Yes, I--"

"But you mustn't!--you ain't strong enough!--you'll fall!--there's nothin' there!" they exclaimed wildly, talking both together and hurrying forward.

"Oh, I guess 't won't kill me," said the old woman; and something in the tone of her voice made them fall back. They were still staring into each other's eyes when the hall door closed sharply behind her.

"It's all--up!" breathed Jim.

Fully fifteen minutes passed before the old woman came back. She entered the room quietly, and limped across the floor to the chair by the window.

"It's real pretty," she said. "I allers did like gray."

"Gray?" stammered Ella.

"Yes!--fer coffins, ye know." Jim made a sudden movement, and started to speak; but the old woman raised her hand. "You don't need ter say anythin'," she interposed cheerfully. "I jest wanted ter make sure where 'twas, so I went up. You see, Jed's comin' home, an' I thought he might feel--queer if he run on to it, casual-like."

"Jed--comin' home!"

The old woman smiled oddly.

"Oh, I didn't tell ye, did I? The doctor had this telegram yesterday, an' brought it over to me. Ye know he was here last night. Read it." And she pulled from her pocket a crumpled slip of paper. And Jim read:

Shall be there the 8th. For God's sake don't let me be too late.

J. D. Darling

ACROSS THE YEARS BY ELEANOR H. PORTER

Wristers for Three

The great chair, sumptuous with satin-damask and soft with springs, almost engulfed the tiny figure of the little old lady. To the old lady herself it suddenly seemed the very embodiment of the luxurious ease against which she was so impotently battling. With a spasmodic movement she jerked herself to her feet, and stood there motionless save for the wistful sweep of her eyes about the room.

A level ray from the setting sun shot through the window, gilding the silver of her hair and deepening the faint pink of her cheek; on the opposite wall it threw a sharp silhouette of the alert little figure--that figure which even the passage of years had been able to bend so very little to its will. For a moment the lace kerchief folded across the black gown rose and fell tumultuously; then its wearer crossed the room and seated herself with uncompromising discomfort in the only straight-backed chair the room contained. This done, Mrs. Nancy Wetherby, for the twentieth time, went over in her mind the whole matter.

For two weeks, now, she had been a member of her son John's family--two vain, unprofitable weeks. When before that had the sunset found her night after night with hands limp from a long day of idleness? When before that had the sunrise found her morning after morning with a mind destitute of worthy aim or helpful plan for the coming twelve hours? When, indeed?

Not in her girlhood, not even in her childhood, had there been days of such utter uselessness--rag dolls and mud pies need some care! As for her married life, there were Eben, the babies, the house, the church--and how absolutely necessary she had been to each one!

The babies had quickly grown to stalwart men and sweet-faced women who had as quickly left the home nest and built new nests of their own. Eben had died; and the church--strange how long and longer still the walk to the church had grown each time she had walked it this last year! After all, perhaps it did not matter; there were new faces at the church, and young, strong hands that did not falter and tremble over these new ways of doing things. For a time there had been only the house that needed her--but how great that need had been! There were the rooms to care for, there was the linen to air, there were the dear treasures of picture and toy to cry and laugh over; and outside there were the roses to train and the pansies to pick.

Now, even the house was not left. It was October, and son John had told her that winter was coming on and she must not remain alone. He had brought her to his own great house and placed her in these beautiful rooms--indeed, son John was most kind to her! If only she could make some return, do something, be of some use!

Her heart failed her as she thought of the grave-faced, preoccupied man who came each morning into the room with the question, "Well, mother, is there anything you need to-day?" What possible service could she render him? Her heart failed her again as she thought of John's pretty, new wife, and of the two big boys, men grown, sons of dear dead Molly. There was the baby, to be sure; but the baby was always attended by one, and maybe two, white-capped, white-aproned young women. Madam Wetherby never felt quite sure of herself when with those young women. There were other young women, too, in whose presence she felt equally ill at ease; young women in still prettier white aprons and still daintier white caps; young women who moved noiselessly in and out of the halls and parlors and who waited at table each day.

Was there not some spot, some creature, some thing, in all that place that needed the touch of her hand, the glance of her eye? Surely the day had not quite come when she could be of no use, no service to her kind! Her work must be waiting; she had only to find it. She would seek it out--and that at once. No more of this slothful waiting for the work to come to her! "Indeed, no!" she finished aloud, her dim eyes alight, her breath coming short and quick, and her whole frail self quivering with courage and excitement.

It was scarcely nine o'clock the next morning when a quaint little figure in a huge gingham apron (slyly abstracted from the bottom of a trunk) slipped out of the rooms given over to the use of John Wetherby's mother. The little figure tripped softly, almost stealthily, along the hall and down the wide main staircase. There was some hesitation and there were a few false moves before the rear stairway leading to the kitchen was gained; and there was a gasp, half triumphant, half dismayed, when the kitchen was reached.

The cook stared, open-mouthed, as though confronted with an apparition. A maid, hurrying across the room with a loaded tray, almost dropped her burden to the floor. There was a dazed moment of silence, then Madam Wetherby took a faltering step forward and spoke.

"Good-morning! I--I've come to help you."

"Ma'am!" gasped the cook.

"To help--to help!" nodded the little old lady briskly, with a sudden overwhelming joy at the near prospect of the realization of her hopes. "Pare apples, beat eggs, or--anything!"

"Indeed, ma'am, I--you--" The cook stopped helplessly, and eyed with frightened fascination the little old lady as she crossed to the table and picked up a pan of potatoes.

"Now a knife, please,--oh, here's one," continued Madam Wetherby happily. "Go right about something else. I'll sit over there in that chair, and I'll have these peeled very soon."

When John Wetherby visited his mother's rooms that morning he found no one there to greet him. A few sharp inquiries disclosed the little lady's whereabouts and sent Margaret Wetherby with flaming cheeks and tightening lips into the kitchen.

"Mother!" she cried; and at the word the knife dropped from the trembling, withered old fingers and clattered to the floor. "Why, mother!"

"I--I was helping," quavered a deprecatory voice.

Something in the appealing eyes sent a softer curve to Margaret Wetherby's lips.

"Yes, mother; that was very kind of you," said John's wife gently. "But such work is quite too hard for you, and there's no need of your doing it. Nora will finish these," she added, lifting the pan of potatoes to the table, "and you and I will go upstairs to your room. Perhaps we'll go driving by and by. Who knows?"

In thinking it over afterwards Nancy Wetherby could find no fault with her daughter-in-law. Margaret had been goodness itself, insisting only that such work was not for a moment to be thought of. John's wife was indeed kind, acknowledged Madam Wetherby to herself, yet two big tears welled to her eyes and were still moist on her cheeks after she had fallen asleep.

It was perhaps three days later that John Wetherby's mother climbed the long flight of stairs near her sitting-room door, and somewhat timidly entered one of the airy, sunlit rooms devoted to Master Philip Wetherby. The young woman in attendance respectfully acknowledged her greeting, and Madam Wetherby advanced with some show of courage to the middle of the room.

"The baby, I--I heard him cry," she faltered.

"Yes, madam," smiled the nurse. "It is Master Philip's nap hour."

Louder and louder swelled the wails from the inner room, yet the nurse did not stir save to reach for her thread.

"But he's crying--yet!" gasped Madam Wetherby.

The girl's lips twitched and an expression came to her face which the little old lady did not in the least understand.

"Can't you--do something?" demanded baby's grandmother, her voice shaking.

"No, madam. I--" began the girl, but she did not finish. The little figure before her drew itself to the full extent of its diminutive height.

"Well, I can," said Madam Wetherby crisply. Then she turned and hurried into the inner room.

The nurse sat mute and motionless until a crooning lullaby and the unmistakable tapping of rockers on a bare floor brought her to her feet in dismay. With an angry frown she strode across the room, but she stopped short at the sight that met her eyes.

In a low chair, her face aglow with the accumulated love of years of baby-brooding, sat the little old lady, one knotted, wrinkled finger tightly elapsed within a dimpled fist. The cries had dropped to sobbing breaths, and the lullaby, feeble and quavering though it was, rose and swelled triumphant. The anger fled from the girl's face, and a queer choking came to her throat so that her words were faint and broken.

"Madam--I beg pardon--I'm sorry, but I must put Master Philip back on his bed."

"But he isn't asleep yet," demurred Madam Wetherby softly, her eyes mutinous.

"But you must--I can't--that is, Master Philip cannot be rocked," faltered the girl.

"Nonsense, my dear!" she said; "babies can always be rocked!" And again the lullaby rose on the air.

"But, madam," persisted the girl--she was almost crying now--"don't you see? I must put Master Philip back. It is Mrs. Wetherby's orders. They-- they don't rock babies so much now."

For an instant fierce rebellion spoke through flashing eyes, stern-set lips, and tightly clutched fingers; then all the light died from the thin old face and the tense muscles relaxed.

"You may put the baby back," said Madam Wetherby tremulously, yet with a sudden dignity that set the maid to curtsying. "I--I should not want to cross my daughter's wishes."

Nancy Wetherby never rocked her grandson again, but for days she haunted the nursery, happy if she could but tie the baby's moccasins or hold his brush or powder-puff; yet a week had scarcely passed when John's wife said to her:

"Mother, dear, I wouldn't tire myself so trotting upstairs each day to the nursery. There isn't a bit of need--Mary and Betty can manage quite well. You fatigue yourself too much!" And to the old lady's denials John's wife returned, with a tinge of sharpness: "But, really, mother, I'd rather you didn't. It frets the nurses and--forgive me--but you know you will forget and talk to him in 'baby-talk'!"

The days came and the days went, and Nancy Wetherby stayed more and more closely to her rooms. She begged one day for the mending-basket, but her daughter-in-law laughed and kissed her.

"Tut, tut, mother, dear!" she remonstrated. "As if I'd have you wearing your eyes and fingers out mending a paltry pair of socks!"

"Then I--I'll knit new ones!" cried the old lady, with sudden inspiration.

"Knit new ones--stockings!" laughed Margaret Wetherby. "Why, dearie, they never in this world would wear them--and if they would, I couldn't let you do it," she added gently, as she noted the swift clouding of the eager face. "Such tiresome work!"

Again the old eyes filled with tears; and yet--John's wife was kind, so very kind!

It was a cheerless, gray December morning that John Wetherby came into his mother's room and found a sob-shaken little figure in the depths of the sumptuous, satin-damask chair. "Mother, mother,--why, mother!" There were amazement and real distress in John Wetherby's voice.

"There, there, John, I--I didn't mean to--truly I didn't!" quavered the little old lady.

John dropped on one knee and caught the fluttering fingers. "Mother, what is it?"

"It--it isn't anything; truly it isn't," urged the tremulous voice.

"Is any one unkind to you?" John's eyes grew stern. "The boys, or-- Margaret?"

The indignant red mounted to the faded cheek. "John! How can you ask? Every one is kind, kind, so very kind to me!"

"Well, then, what is it?"

There was only a sob in reply. "Come, come," he coaxed gently.

For a moment Nancy Wetherby's breath was held suspended, then it came in a burst with a rush of words.

"Oh, John, John, I'm so useless, so useless, so dreadfully useless! Don't you see? Not a thing, not a person needs me. The kitchen has the cook and the maids. The baby has two or three nurses. Not even this room needs me--there's a girl to dust it each day. Once I slipped out of bed and did it first--I did, John; but she came in, and when I told her, she just curtsied and smiled and kept right on, and--she didn't even skip one chair! John, dear John, sometimes it seems as though even my own self doesn't need me. I--I don't even put on my clothes alone; there's always some one to help me!"

"There, there, dear," soothed the man huskily. "I need you, indeed I do, mother." And he pressed his lips to one, then the other, of the wrinkled, soft-skinned hands.

"You don't--you don't!" choked the woman. "There's not one thing I can do for you! Why, John, only think, I sit with idle hands all day, and there was so much once for them to do. There was Eben, and the children, and the house, and the missionary meetings, and--"

On and on went the sweet old voice, but the man scarcely heard. Only one phrase rang over and over in his ears, "There's not one thing I can do for you!" All the interests of now--stocks, bonds, railroads--fell from his mind and left it blank save for the past. He was a boy again at his mother's knee. And what had she done for him then? Surely among all the myriad things there must be one that he might single out and ask her to do for him now! And yet, as he thought, his heart misgave him.

There were pies baked, clothes made, bumped foreheads bathed, lost pencils found; there were--a sudden vision came to him of something warm and red and very soft--

something over which his boyish heart had exulted. The next moment his face lighted with joy very like that of the years long ago.

"Mother!" he cried. "I know what you can do for me. I want a pair of wristers--red ones, just like those you used to knit!"

It must have been a month later that John Wetherby, with his two elder sons, turned the first corner that carried him out of sight of his house. Very slowly, and with gentle fingers, he pulled off two bright red wristers. He folded them, patted them, then tucked them away in an inner pocket.

"Bless her dear heart!" he said softly. "You should have seen her eyes shine when I put them on this morning!"

"I can imagine it," said one of his sons in a curiously tender voice. The other one smiled, and said whimsically, "I can hardly wait for mine!" Yet even as he spoke his eyes grew dim with a sudden moisture.

Back at the house John's mother was saying to John's wife: "Did you see them on him, Margaret?--John's wristers? They did look so bright and pretty! And I'm to make more, too; did you know? Frank and Edward want some; John said so. He told them about his, and they wanted some right away. Only think, Margaret," she finished, lifting with both hands the ball of red worsted and pressing it close to her cheek, "I've got two whole pairs to make now!"

The Giving Thanks of Cyrus and Huldah

For two months Cyrus Gregg and his wife Huldah had not spoken to each other, yet all the while they had lived under the same roof, driven to church side by side, and attended various festivities and church prayer-meetings together.

The cause of the quarrel had been an insignificant something that speedily lost itself in the torrent of angry words that burst from the lips of the irate husband and wife, until by night it would have been difficult for either the man or the woman to tell exactly what had been the first point of difference. By that time, however, the quarrel had assumed such proportions that it loomed in their lives larger than anything else; and each had vowed never to speak to the other until that other had made the advance.

On both sides they came of a stubborn race, and from the first it was a battle royally fought. The night of the quarrel Cyrus betook himself in solitary state to the "spare-room" over the parlor. After that he slept on a makeshift bed that he had prepared for himself in the shed-chamber, hitherto sacred to trunks, dried corn, and cobwebs.

For a month the two sat opposite to each other and partook of Huldah's excellent cooking; then one day the woman found at her plate a piece--of brown paper on which had been scrawled:

If I ain't worth speakin' to I ain't worth cookin' for. Hereafter I'll take care of myself.

A day later came the retort. Cyrus found it tucked under the shed-chamber door.

Huldah's note showed her "schooling." It was well written, carefully spelled, and enclosed in a square white envelope.

Sir [it ran stiffly]: I shall be obliged if you do not chop any more wood for me. Hereafter I shall use the oil stove. HULDAH PENDLETON GREGG.

Cyrus choked, and peered at the name with suddenly blurred eyes: the "Huldah Pendleton" was fiercely black and distinct; the "Gregg" was so faint it could scarcely be discerned.

"Why, it's 'most like a d'vorce!" he shivered.

If it had not been so pitiful, it would have been ludicrous--what followed. Day after day, in one corner of the kitchen, an old man boiled his potatoes and fried his unappetizing eggs over a dusty, unblacked stove; in the other corner an old woman baked and brewed over a shining idol of brass and black enamel--and always the baking and brewing carried to the nostrils of the hungry man across the room the aroma of some dainty that was a particular favorite of his own.

The man whistled, and the woman hummed--at times; but they did not talk, except when some neighbor came in; and then they both talked very loud and very fast--to the neighbor. On this one point were Cyrus Gregg and his wife Huldah agreed; under no circumstances whatever must any gossiping outsider know.

One by one the weeks had passed. It was November now, and very cold. Outdoors a dull gray sky and a dull brown earth combined into a dismal hopelessness. Indoors the dull monotony of a two-months-old quarrel and a growing heartache made a combination that carried even less of cheer.

Huldah never hummed now, and Cyrus seldom whistled; yet neither was one whit nearer speaking. Each saw this, and, curiously enough, was pleased. In fact, it was just here that, in spite of the heartache, each found an odd satisfaction.

"By sugar--but she's a spunky one!" Cyrus would chuckle admiringly, as he discovered some new evidence of his wife's shrewdness in obtaining what she wanted with yet no spoken word.

"There isn't another man in town who could do it--and stick to it!" exulted Huldah proudly, her eyes on her husband's form, bent over his egg-frying at the other side of the room.

Not only the cause of the quarrel, but almost the quarrel itself, had now long since been forgotten; in fact, to both Cyrus and his wife it had come to be a sort of game in which each player watched the other's progress with fully as much interest as he did his own. And yet, with it all there was the heartache; for the question came to them at times with sickening force--just when and how could it possibly end?

It was at about this time that each began to worry about the other. Huldah shuddered at the changeless fried eggs and boiled potatoes; and Cyrus ordered a heavy storm window for the room where Huldah slept alone. Huldah slyly left a new apple pie almost under her husband's nose one day, and Cyrus slipped a five-dollar bill beneath his wife's napkin ring. When both pie and greenback remained untouched, Huldah cried, and Cyrus said, "Gosh darn it!" three times in succession behind the woodshed door.

A week before Thanksgiving a letter came from the married daughter, and another from the married son. They were good letters, kind and loving; and each closed with a suggestion that all go home at Thanksgiving for a family reunion.

Huldah read the letters eagerly, but at their close she frowned and looked anxious. In a moment she had passed them to Cyrus with a toss of her head. Five minutes later Cyrus had flung them back with these words trailing across one of the envelopes:

Write um. Tell um we are sick--dead--gone away--anything! Only don't let um come. A if we wanted to Thanksgive!
Huldah answered the letters that night. She, too, wrote kindly and lovingly; but at the end she said that much as she and father would like to see them, it did not seem wise to undertake to entertain such a family gathering just now. It would be better to postpone it.

Both Huldah and Cyrus hoped that this would end the subject of Thanksgiving; but it did not. The very next day Cyrus encountered neighbor Wiley in the village store. Wiley's round red face shone like the full moon.

"Well, well, Cy, what ye doin' down your way Thanksgivin'--eh?" he queried.

Cyrus stiffened; but before he could answer he discovered that Wiley had asked the question, not for information, but as a mere introduction to a recital of his own plans.

"We're doin' great things," announced the man. "Sam an' Jennie an' the hull kit on 'em's comin' home an' bring all the chicks. Tell ye what, Cy, we be a-Thanksgivin' this year! Ain't nothin' like a good old fam'ly reunion, when ye come right down to it."

"Yes, I know," said Cyrus gloomily. "But we--we ain't doin' much this year."

A day later came Huldah's turn. She had taken some calf's-foot jelly to Mrs. Taylor in the little house at the foot of the hill. The Widow Taylor was crying.

"You see, it's Thanksgiving!" she sobbed, in answer to Huldah's dismayed questions.

"Thanksgiving!"

"Yes. And last year I had--him!"

Huldah sighed, and murmured something comforting, appropriate; but almost at once she stopped, for the woman had turned searching eyes upon her.

"Huldah Gregg, do you appreciate Cyrus?"

Huldah bridled angrily, but there was no time for a reply, for the woman answered her own question, and hurried on wildly.

"No. Did I appreciate my husband? No. Does Sally Clark appreciate her husband? No. And there don't none of us do it till he's gone--gone-- gone!"

As soon as possible Huldah went home. She was not a little disconcerted. The "gone--gone--gone" rang unpleasantly in her ears, and before her eyes rose a hateful vision of unappetizing fried eggs and boiled potatoes. As to her not appreciating Cyrus--that was all nonsense; she had always appreciated him, and that, too, far beyond his just deserts, she told herself angrily.

There was no escaping Thanksgiving after that for either Huldah or Cyrus. It looked from every eager eye, and dropped from every joyous lip, until, of all the world Huldah and Cyrus came to regard themselves as the most forlorn, and the most abused.

It was then that to Huldah came her great idea; she would cook for Cyrus the best Thanksgiving dinner he had ever eaten. Just because he was obstinate was no reason why he should starve, she told herself; and very gayly she set about carrying out her plans. First the oil stove, with the help of a jobman, was removed to the unfinished room over the kitchen, for the chief charm of the dinner was to be its secret preparation. Then, with the treasured butter-and-egg money the turkey, cranberries, nuts, and raisins were bought and smuggled into the house and upstairs to the chamber of mystery.

Two days before Thanksgiving Cyrus came home to find a silent and almost empty kitchen. His heart skipped a beat and his jaw fell open in frightened amazement; then a step on the floor above sent the blood back to his face and a new bitterness to his heart.

"So I ain't even good enough ter stay with!" he muttered. "Fool!--fool!" he snarled, glaring at the oblong brown paper in his arms. "As if she'd care for this--now!" he finished, flinging the parcel into the farthest corner of the room.

Unhappy Cyrus! To him, also, had come a great idea. Thanksgiving was not Christmas, to be sure, but if he chose to give presents on that day, surely it was no one's business but his own, he argued. In the brown paper parcel at that moment lay the soft, shimmering folds of yards upon yards of black silk--and Huldah had been longing for a new black silk gown. Yet it was almost dark when Cyrus stumbled over to the corner, picked up the parcel, and carried it ruefully away to the shed-chamber.

Thanksgiving dawned clear and unusually warm. The sun shone, and the air felt like spring. The sparrows twittered in the treetops as if the branches were green with leaves.

To Cyrus, however, it was a world of gloom. Upstairs Huldah was singing-- singing!-- and it was Thanksgiving. He could hear her feet patter, patter on the floor above, and the sound had a cheery self-reliance that was maddening. Huldah was happy, evidently--and it was Thanksgiving! Twice he had walked resolutely to the back stairs with a brown-paper parcel in his arms; and twice a quavering song of triumph from the room above had sent him back in defeat. As if she could care for a present of his!

Suddenly, now, Cyrus sprang forward in his chair, sniffing the air hungrily. Turkey! Huldah was roasting turkey, while he--

The old man dropped back in his seat and turned his eyes disconsolately on the ill-kept stove--fried eggs and boiled potatoes are not the most toothsome prospect for a Thanksgiving dinner, particularly when one has the smell of a New England housewife's turkey in one's nostrils.

For a time Cyrus sat motionless; then he rose to his feet, shuffled out of the house, and across the road to the barn.

In the room above the kitchen, at that moment, something happened. Perhaps the old hands slipped in their eagerness, or perhaps the old eyes judged a distance wrongly. Whatever it was, there came a puff of smoke, a sputter, and a flare of light; then red-yellow flames leaped to the flimsy shade at the window, and swept on to the century-seasoned timbers above.

With a choking cry, Huldah turned and stumbled across the room to the stairway. Out at the barn door Cyrus, too, saw the flare of light at the window, and he, too, turned with a choking cry.

They met at the foot of the stairway.

"Huldah!"

"Cyrus!"

It was as if one voice had spoken, so exactly were the words simultaneous. Then Cyrus cried:

"You ain't hurt?"

"No, no! Quick--the things--we must get them out!"

Obediently Cyrus turned and began to work; and the first thing that his arms tenderly bore to safety was an oblong brown-paper parcel.

From all directions then came the neighbors running. The farming settlement was miles from a town or a fire-engine. The house was small, and stood quite by itself; and there was little, after all, that could be done, except to save the household goods and gods. This was soon accomplished, and there was nothing to do but to watch the old house burn.

Cyrus and Huldah sat hand in hand on an old stone wall, quite apart from their sympathetic neighbors, and--talked. And about them was a curious air of elation, a buoyancy as if long-pent forces had suddenly found a joyous escape.

"'T ain't as if our things wan't all out," cried Cyrus; his voice was actually exultant.

"Or as if we hadn't wanted to build a new one for years," chirruped his wife.

"Now you can have that 'ere closet under the front stairs, Huldah!"

"And you can have the room for your tools where it'll be warm in the winter!"

"An' there'll be the bow-winder out of the settin' room, Huldah!"

"Yes, and a real bathroom, with water coming right out of the wall, same as the Wileys have!"

"An' a tub, Huldah--one o' them pretty white chiny ones!"

"Oh, Cyrus, ain't it almost too good to be true!" sighed Huldah: then her face changed. "Why, Cyrus, it's gone," she cried with sudden sharpness.

"What's gone?"

"Your dinner--I was cooking such a beautiful turkey and all the fixings for you."

A dull red came into the man's face.

"For--me?" stammered Cyrus.

"Y-yes," faltered Huldah; then her chin came up defiantly.

The man laughed; and there was a boyish ring to his voice.

"Well, Huldah, I didn't have any turkey, but I did have a tidy little piece o' black silk for yer gown, an' I saved it, too. Mebbe we could eat that!--eh?"

It was not until just as they were falling asleep that night in Deacon Clark's spare bedroom that Mr. and Mrs. Gregg so much as hinted that there ever had been a quarrel.

Then, under cover of the dark, Cyrus stammered:

"Huldah, did ye sense it? Them 'ere words we said at the foot of the stairs was spoke--exactly--together!"

"Yes, I know, dear," murmured Huldah, with a little break in her voice. Then:

"Cyrus, ain't it wonderful--this Thanksgiving, for us?"

Downstairs the Clarks were talking of poor old Mr. and Mrs. Gregg and their "sad loss;" but the Clarks did not--know.

A New England Idol

The Hapgood twins were born in the great square house that set back from the road just on the outskirts of Fairtown. Their baby eyes had opened upon a world of faded portraits and somber haircloth furniture, and their baby hands had eagerly clutched at crystal pendants on brass candlesticks gleaming out of the sacred darkness that enveloped the parlor mantel.

When older grown they had played dolls in the wonderful attic, and made mud pies in the wilderness of a back yard. The garden had been a fairyland of delight to their toddling feet, and the apple trees a fragrant shelter for their first attempts at housekeeping.

From babyhood to girlhood the charm of the old place grew upon them, so much so that the thought of leaving it for homes of their own became distasteful to them, and they looked with scant favor upon the occasional village youths who sauntered up the path presumably on courtship bent.

The Reverend John Hapgood--a man who ruled himself and all about him with the iron rod of a rigid old-school orthodoxy--died when the twins were twenty; and the frail little woman who, as his wife, had for thirty years lived and moved solely because he expected breath and motion of her, followed soon in his footsteps. And then the twins were left alone in the great square house on the hill.

Miss Tabitha and Miss Rachel were not the only children of the family. There had been a son--the first born, and four years their senior. The headstrong boy and the iron rule had clashed, and the boy, when sixteen years old, had fled, leaving no trace behind him.

If the Reverend John Hapgood grieved for his wayward son the members of his household knew it not, save as they might place their own constructions on the added sternness to his eyes and the deepening lines about his mouth. "Paul," when it designated the graceless runaway, was a forbidden word in the family, and even the Epistles in the sacred Book, bearing the prohibited name, came to be avoided by the head of the house in the daily readings. It was still music in the hearts of the women, however, though it never passed their lips; and when the little mother lay dying she remembered and spoke of her boy. The habit of years still fettered her tongue and kept it from uttering the name.

"If--he--comes--you know--if he comes, be kind--be good," she murmured, her breath short and labored. "Don't--punish," she whispered--he was yet a lad in her disordered vision. "Don't punish--forgive!"

Years had passed since then--years of peaceful mornings and placid afternoons, and Paul had never appeared. Each purpling of the lilacs in the spring and reddening of the apples in the fall took on new shades of loveliness in the fond eyes of the twins, and every blade of grass and tiny shrub became sacred to them.

On the 10th of June, their thirty-fifth birthday, the place never had looked so lovely. A small table laid with spotless linen and gleaming silver stood beneath the largest apple-tree, a mute witness that the ladies were about to celebrate their birthday--the 10th of June being the only day that the solemn dignity of the dining-room was deserted for the frivolous freedom of the lawn.

Rachel came out of the house and sniffed the air joyfully.

"Delicious!" she murmured. "Somehow, the 10th of June is specially fine every year."

In careful, uplifted hands she bore a round frosted cake, always the chief treasure of the birthday feast. The cake was covered with the tiny colored candies so dear to the heart of a child. Miss Rachel always bought those candies at the village store, with the apology:--

"I want them for Tabitha's birthday cake, you know. She thinks so much of pretty things."

Tabitha invariably made the cake and iced it, and as she dropped the bits of colored sugar into place, she would explain to Huldy, who occasionally "helped" in the kitchen:--

"I wouldn't miss the candy for the world--my sister thinks so much of it!"

So each deceived herself with this pleasant bit of fiction, and yet had what she herself most wanted.

Rachel carefully placed the cake in the center of the table, feasted her eyes on its toothsome loveliness, then turned and hurried back to the house. The door had scarcely shut behind her when a small, ragged urchin darted in at the street gate, snatched the cake, and, at a sudden sound from the house, dashed out of sight behind a shrub close by.

The sound that had frightened the boy was the tapping of the heels of Miss Tabitha's shoes along the back porch. The lady descended the steps, crossed the lawn and placed a saucer of pickles and a plate of dainty sandwiches on the table.

"Why, I thought Rachel brought the cake," she said aloud. "It must be in the house; there's other things to get, anyway. I'll go back."

Again the click of the door brought the small boy close to the table. Filling both hands with sandwiches, he slipped behind the shrub just as the ladies came out of the house together. Rachel carried a small tray laden with sauce and tarts; Tabitha, one with water and steaming tea. As they neared the table each almost dropped her burden.

"Why, where's my cake?"

"And my sandwiches?"

"There's the plate it was on!" Rachel's voice was growing in terror.

"And mine, too!" cried Tabitha, with distended eyes fastened on some bits of bread and meat--all that the small brown hands had left.

"It's burglars--robbers!" Rachel looked furtively over her shoulder.

"And all your lovely cake!" almost sobbed Tabitha.

"It--it was yours, too," said the other with a catch in her voice. "Oh, dear! What can have happened to it? I never heard of such a thing--right in broad daylight!" The sisters had long ago set their trays upon the ground and were now wringing their hands helplessly. Suddenly a small figure appeared before them holding out four sadly crushed sandwiches and half of a crumbling cake.

"I'm sorry--awful sorry! I didn't think--I was so hungry. I'm afraid there ain't very much left," he added, with rueful eyes on the sandwiches.

"No, I should say not!" vouchsafed Rachel, her voice firm now that the size of the "burglar" was declared. Tabitha only gasped.

The small boy placed the food upon the empty plates, and Rachel's lips twitched as she saw that he clumsily tried to arrange it in an orderly fashion.

"There, ma'am,--that looks pretty good!" he finally announced with some pride.

Tabitha made an involuntary gesture of aversion. Rachel laughed outright; then her face grew suddenly stern.

"Boy, what do you mean by such actions?" she demanded.

His eyes fell, and his cheeks showed red through the tan.

"I was hungry."

"But didn't you know it was stealing?" she asked, her face softening.

"I didn't stop to think--it looked so good I couldn't help takin' it." He dug his bare toes in the grass for a moment in silence, then he raised his head with a jerk and stood squarely on both feet. "I hain't got any money, but I'll work to pay for it--bringin' wood in, or somethin'."

"The dear child!" murmured two voices softly.

"I've got to find my folks, sometime, but I'll do the work first. Mebbe an hour'll pay for it--'most!"--He looked hopefully into Miss Rachel's face.

"Who are your folks?" she asked huskily.

By way of answer he handed out a soiled, crumpled envelope for her inspection on which was written, "Reverend John Hapgood."

"Why--it's father!"

"What!" exclaimed Tabitha.

Her sister tore the note open with shaking fingers.

"It's from--Paul!" she breathed, hesitating a conscientious moment over the name. Then she turned her startled eyes on the boy, who was regarding her with lively interest.

"Do I belong to you?" he asked anxiously.

"I--I don't know. Who are you--what's your name?"

"Ralph Hapgood."

Tabitha had caught up the note and was devouring it with swift-moving eyes.

"It's Paul's boy, Rachel," she broke in, "only think of it--Paul's boy!" and she dropped the bit of paper and enveloped the lad in a fond but tearful embrace.

He squirmed uneasily.

"I'm sorry I eat up my own folks's things. I'll go to work any time," he suggested, trying to draw away, and wiping a tear splash from the back of his hand on his trousers.

But it was long hours before Ralph Hapgood was allowed to "go to work." Tears, kisses, embraces, questions, a bath, and clean clothes followed each other in quick succession-- the clothes being some of his own father's boyhood garments.

His story was quickly told. His mother was long since dead, and his father had written on his dying bed the letter that commended the boy-- so soon to be orphaned--to the pity and care of his grandparents. The sisters trembled and changed color at the story of the boy's hardships on the way to Fairtown; and they plied him with questions and sandwiches in about equal proportions after he told of the frequent dinnerless days and supperless nights of the journey.

That evening when the boy was safe in bed--clean, full-stomached, and sleepily content the sisters talked it over. The Reverend John Hapgood, in his will, had cut off his recreant son with the proverbial shilling, so, by law, there was little coming to Ralph. This, however, the sisters overlooked in calm disdain.

"We must keep him, anyhow," said Rachel with decision.

"Yes, indeed,--the dear child!"

"He's twelve, for all he's so small, but he hasn't had much schooling. We must see to that--we want him well educated," continued Rachel, a pink spot showing in either cheek.

"Indeed we do--we'll send him to college! I wonder, now, wouldn't he like to be a doctor?"

"Perhaps," admitted the other cautiously, "or a minister."

"Sure enough--he might like that better; I'm going to ask him!" and she sprang to her feet and tripped across the room to the parlor-bedroom door. "Ralph," she called softly, after turning the knob, "are you asleep?"

"Huh? N-no, ma'am." The voice nearly gave the lie to the words.

"Well, dear, we were wondering--would you rather be a minister or a doctor?" she asked, much as though she were offering for choice a peach and a pear.

"A doctor!" came emphatically from out of the dark--there was no sleep in the voice now. "I've always wanted to be a doctor."

"You shall, oh, you shall!" promised the woman ecstatically, going back to her sister; and from that time all their lives were ordered with that one end in view.

The Hapgood twins were far from wealthy. They owned the homestead, but their income was small, and the added mouth to fill--and that a hungry one--counted. As the years passed, Huldy came less and less frequently to help in the kitchen, and the sisters' gowns grew more and more rusty and darned.

Ralph, boylike, noticed nothing--indeed, half the year he was away at school; but as the time drew near for the college course and its attendant expenses, the sisters were sadly troubled.

"We might sell," suggested Tabitha, a little choke in her voice.

Rachel started.

"Why, sister!--sell? Oh, no, we couldn't do that!" she shuddered.

"But what can we do?"

"Do?--why lots of things!" Rachel's lips came together with a snap. "It's coming berry time, and there's our chickens, and the garden did beautifully last year. Then there's your lace work and my knitting-- they bring something. Sell? Oh--we couldn't do that!" And she abruptly left the room and went out into the yard. There she lovingly trained a wayward vine with new shoots going wrong, and gloated over the rosebushes heavy with crimson buds.

But as the days and weeks flew by and September drew the nearer, Rachel's courage failed her. Berries had been scarce, the chickens had died, the garden had suffered from drought, and but for their lace and knitting work, their income would have dwindled to a pitiful sum indeed. Ralph had been gone all summer; he had asked to go camping and fishing with some of his school friends. He was expected home a week before the college opened, however.

Tabitha grew more and more restless every day. Finally she spoke.

"Rachel, we'll have to sell--there isn't any other way. It would bring a lot," she continued hurriedly, before her sister could speak, "and we could find some pretty rooms somewhere. It wouldn't be so very dreadful!"

"Don't, Tabitha! Seems as though I couldn't bear even to speak of it. Sell?--oh, Tabitha!" Then her voice changed from a piteous appeal to one of forced conviction.

"We couldn't get anywhere near what it's worth, Tabitha, anyway. No one here wants it or can afford to buy it for what it ought to bring. It is really absurd to think of it. Of course, if I had an offer--a good big one--that would be quite another thing; but there's no hope of that."

Rachel's lips said "hope," but her heart said "danger," and the latter was what she really meant. She did not know that but two hours before, a stranger had said to a Fairtown lawyer:

"I want a summer home in this locality. You don't happen to know of a good old treasure of a homestead for sale, do you?"

"I do not," replied the lawyer. "There's a place on the edge of the village that would be just the ticket, but I don't suppose it could be bought for love nor money."

"Where is it?" asked the man eagerly. "You never know what money can do-- to say nothing of love--till you try."

The lawyer chuckled softly.

"It's the Hapgood place. I'll drive you over to-morrow. It's owned by two old maids, and they worship every stick and stone and blade of grass that belongs to it. However, I happen to know that cash is rather scarce with them--and there's ample chance for love, if the money fails," he added, with a twitching of his lips.

When the two men drove into the yard that August morning, the Hapgood twins were picking nasturtiums, and the flaming yellows and scarlets lighted up their somber gowns, and made patches of brilliant color against the gray of the house.

"By Jove, it's a picture!" exclaimed the would-be purchaser.

The lawyer smiled and sprang to the ground. Introductions swiftly followed, then he cleared his throat in some embarrassment.

"Ahem! I've brought Mr. Hazelton up here, ladies, because he was interested in your beautiful place."

Miss Rachel smiled--the smile of proud possession; then something within her seemed to tighten, and she caught her breath sharply.

"It is fine!" murmured Hazelton; "and the view is grand!" he continued, his eyes on the distant hills. Then he turned abruptly. "Ladies, I believe in coming straight to the point. I want a summer home, and--I want this one. Can I tempt you to part with it?"

"Indeed, no!" began Rachel almost fiercely. Then her voice sank to a whisper; "I--I don't think you could."

"But, sister," interposed Tabitha, her face alight, "you know you said-- that is, there are circumstances--perhaps he would--p-pay enough--" Her voice stumbled over the hated word, then stopped, while her face burned scarlet.

"Pay!--no human mortal could pay for this house!" flashed Rachel indignantly. Then she turned to Hazelton, her slight form drawn to its greatest height, and her hands crushing the flowers, she held till the brittle stems snapped, releasing a fluttering shower of scarlet and gold. "Mr. Hazelton, to carry out certain wishes very near to our hearts, we need money. We will show you the place, and--and we will consider your offer," she finished faintly. It was a dreary journey the sisters took that morning, though the garden never had seemed lovelier, nor the rooms more sacredly beautiful. In the end,

Hazelton's offer was so fabulously enormous to their unwilling ears that their conscience forbade them to refuse it.

"I'll have the necessary papers ready to sign in a few days," said the lawyer as the two gentlemen turned to go. And Hazelton added: "If at any time before that you change your minds and find you cannot give it up-- just let me know and it will be all right. Just think it over till then," he said kindly, the dumb woe in their eyes appealing to him as the loudest lamentations could not have done. "But if you don't mind, I'd like to have an architect, who is in town just now, come up and look it over with me," he finished.

"Certainly, sir, certainly," said Rachel, longing for the man to go. But when he was gone, she wished him back--anything would be better than this aimless wandering from room to room, and from yard to garden and back again.

"I suppose he will sit here," murmured Tabitha, dropping wearily on to the settee under the apple-trees.

"I suppose so," her sister assented. "I wonder if she knows how to grow roses; they'll certainly die if she doesn't!" And Rachel crushed a worm under her foot with unnecessary vigor.

"Oh, I hope they'll tend to the vines on the summerhouse, Rachel, and the pansies--you don't think they'll let them run to seed, do you? Oh, dear!" And Tabitha sprang nervously to her feet and started back to the house.

Mr. Hazelton appeared the next morning with two men--an architect and a landscape gardener. Rachel was in the summerhouse, and the first she knew of their presence was the sound of talking outside.

"You'll want to grade it down there," she heard a strange voice say, "and fill in that little hollow; clear away all those rubbishy posies, and mass your flowering shrubs in the background. Those roses are no particular good, I fancy; we'll move such as are worth anything, and make a rose-bed on the south side--we'll talk over the varieties you want, later. Of course these apple-trees and those lilacs will be cut down, and this summerhouse will be out of the way. You'll be surprised-- a few changes will do wonders, and--"

He stopped abruptly. A woman, tall, flushed, and angry-eyed, stood before him in the path. She opened her lips, but no sound came--Mr. Hazelton was lifting his hat. The flush faded, and her eyes closed as though to shut out some painful sight; then she bowed her head with a proud gesture, and sped along the way to the house.

Once inside, she threw herself, sobbing, upon the bed. Tabitha found her there an hour later.

"You poor dear--they've gone now," she comforted.

Rachel raised her head.

"They're going to cut down everything--every single thing!" she gasped.

"I know it," choked Tabitha, "and they're going to tear out lots of doors inside, and build in windows and things. Oh, Rachel,--what shall we do?"

"I don't know, oh, I don't know!" moaned the woman on the bed, diving into the pillows and hugging them close to her head.

"We--we might give up selling--he said we could if we wanted to."

"But there's Ralph!"

"I know it. Oh, dear--what can we do?"

Rachel suddenly sat upright.

"Do? Why, we'll stand it, of course. We just mustn't mind if he turns the house into a hotel and the yard into a--a pasture!" she said hysterically. "We must just think of Ralph and of his being a doctor. Come, let's go to the village and see if we can rent that tenement of old Mrs. Goddard's."

With a long sigh and a smothered sob, Tabitha went to get her hat.

Mrs. Goddard greeted the sisters effusively, and displayed her bits of rooms and the tiny square of yard with the plainly expressed wish that the place might be their home.

The twins said little, but their eyes were troubled. They left with the promise to think it over and let Mrs. Goddard know.

"I didn't suppose rooms could be so little," whispered Tabitha, as they closed the gate behind them.

"We couldn't grow as much as a sunflower in that yard," faltered Rachel.

"Well, anyhow, we could have some houseplants!"--Tabitha tried to speak cheerfully.

"Indeed we could!" agreed Rachel, rising promptly to her sister's height; "and, after all, little rooms are lots cheaper to heat than big ones." And there the matter ended for the time being.

Mr. Hazelton and the lawyer with the necessary papers appeared a few days later. As the lawyer took off his hat he handed a letter to Miss Rachel.

"I stepped into the office and got your mail," he said genially.

"Thank you," replied the lady, trying to smile. "It's from Ralph,"-- handing it over for her sister to read.

Both the ladies were in somber black; a ribbon or a brooch seemed out of place to them that day. Tabitha broke the seal of the letter, and retired to the light of the window to read it.

The papers were spread on the table, and the pen was in Rachel's hand when a scream from Tabitha shattered the oppressive silence of the room.

"Stop--stop--oh, stop!" she cried, rushing to her sister and snatching the pen from her fingers. "We don't have to--see--read!"--pointing to the postscript written in a round, boyish hand.

Oh, I say, I've got a surprise for you. You think I've been fishing and loafing all summer, but I've been working for the hotels here the whole time. I've got a fine start on my money for college, and I've got a chance to work for my board all this year by helping Professor Heaton. I met him here this summer, and he's the right sort--every time. I've intended all along to help myself a bit when it came to the college racket, but I didn't mean to tell you until I knew I could do it. But it's a sure thing now.

Bye-bye; I'll be home next Saturday.

Your aff. nephew,

Ralph.

Rachel had read this aloud, but her voice ended in a sob instead of in the boy's name. Hazelton brushed the back of his hand across his eyes, and the lawyer looked intently out the window. For a moment there was a silence that could be felt, then Hazelton stepped to the table and fumbled noisily with the papers.

"Ladies, I withdraw my offer," he announced. "I can't afford to buy this house--I can't possibly afford it--it's too expensive." And without another word he left the room, motioning the lawyer to follow.

The sisters looked into each other's eyes and drew a long, sobbing breath.

"Rachel, is it true?"

"Oh, Tabitha! Let's--let's go out under the apple-trees and--just know that they are there!"

And hand in hand they went.

The End